THE MU
BORGO SA

*

Italy in the last days of the war; en route for the
Eighth Army is gallant Major Widdicombe, just
arrived from England, with three cook reinforce-
ments. A slight error takes him to the mountain
village of Borgo San Marco, where he finds himself
cut off from both armies—along with the equally
gallant German Major Trommel and his batman.
As the fortunes of war favour first one side and then
the other in the plain below, the two majors satisfy
military honour by taking each other prisoner and
sharing the spoils of victory, of which the chief one
is the ever-willing Countess of San Marco . . .

W. H. Canaway

The Mules of Borgo San Marco

ARROW BOOKS

ARROW BOOKS LTD
178–202 Great Portland Street, London W1

AN IMPRINT OF THE HUTCHINSON GROUP

London Melbourne Sydney
Auckland Bombay Toronto
Johannesburg New York

✳

First published by
Hutchinson & Co (*Publishers*) Ltd 1967
Arrow edition 1969

*Made and printed in Great Britain
by The Anchor Press Ltd.,
Tiptree, Essex*
09 001560 6

ORNING, early morning, the sun coming up over the far Adriatic to eastward, the foothills turning from shadowed purple to harsh brown, black-hollowed, and then the sudden winding ribbon of the road blazing white where its convolutions were not masked by the shoulders of the hills, the road climbing into the mountains to Borgo San Marco. There the road stopped and sat down upon itself in the main and only square of secretive shuttered houses, an inn with a petrol pump and no petrol and no wine either, a few shops and a barber's, the command post converted from the house next door to the inn. The lower storey had been roughly fortified, and built out from what had been the front door was a concrete blockhouse with slitted machine-gun embrasures dominating the road where it lay beneath the parapet of the square. The command post was deserted. Above the houses and the narrow alleys leading off the square the palazzo hunched, a crenellated stone block with blind shuttered windows.

The inner courtyard of the palazzo lay in shadow that early spring morning. Nineteen forty-five, and a year of promise or disaster, depending on which way you looked at it. Mosses splotched the worn flagstones and grasses pushed out from their interstices. A bucket rattled as

Private Wohlhaber opened the kitchen door and stepped out. He paused briefly, yawning; the yawn momentarily drowned the far-off grumble of heavy gunfire. Wohlhaber trudged along to the fountain, where a marble nymph stood in the basin holding aloft an open-mouthed stone fish. A notice reading *trinkbares Wasser* hung from her neck, concealing her breasts. As a matter of routine Wohlhaber slapped her backside absently and then hauled at a brass handle by the rim of the basin. The fish groaned; Wohlhaber pumped on; the fish gurgled. At length a stream of water gushed from its jaws. Wohlhaber glanced at the reflection from a window opposite, making sure that Major Trommel was watching, then he let go the handle and dived for the bucket, bringing it up beneath the thinning stream just as it ceased: a few drops plinked into the bottom of the bucket. Wohlhaber scratched his head, smiling. He smiled because he knew that without this simulated difficulty over sequential tasks he would still have been at the Russian front instead of Borgo San Marco. He was tall and amiable, with close-cropped fair hair and blue eyes, his field-grey trousers tucked into his socks; he wore neither jacket nor boots, and his shirt-sleeves were rolled up showing strong brown forearms.

'Wohlhaber!'

The expected yell came. Wohlhaber dropped the bucket with a clatter and stiffened to attention, the palms of his hands flat at his sides.

'Turn round.'

Wohlhaber turned, gazing across the courtyard at the opposite wall on which was written *Credere, Obbedire, Combattere* below a tatty painting of a clenched fist and pink, brawny arm, the work of the late Count of San Marco. Wohlhaber mused, his mind wandering. Believe, obey, fight. That was what the old Count had done, from

6

all they said—and that was why he'd snuffed it in Abyssinia. Below the edifying legend a member of a more pragmatic race had written *Dienst ist Dienst und Schnaps ist Schnaps*. That made a deal more sense, except that the booze had all run out.

'Look up, you fool!'

Wohlhaber raised his eyes respectfully to the open window on the second floor and to the bare pigeon-chested torso of Major Trommel; above it the pallid bald head and stringy neck were suddenly flushed by a shaft from the rising sun.

Major Trommel shouted, 'Idiot, how often must I tell you? Now then, listen. On the command "One" you will place the bucket under the spout. On the command "Two" you will commence to pump. On the command "Three" you will desist. Wait for it . . . One!'

Here we go, thought Wohlhaber. He sighed, bent stiffly at the waist, retrieved the bucket and placed it below the jaws of the fish.

'Two!'

He pumped manfully, and the fish groaned, gurgled, gushed; the bucket began to fill.

'Three!'

Wohlhaber's hands dropped to his sides as he stood once more to attention.

'Good,' said Major Trommel. 'Now hurry up with that coffee.'

He closed the window and gazed with complacency at where the Countess lay in bed.

'He's a good man really, you know,' he told her. 'Trouble with him is that one has to spell out things so.'

The Countess yawned, showing thirty-two small white teeth and a pink tongue which curled, flattened and then relaxed as she closed her mouth. She was thirty-eight. She

7

had Titian hair and large black eyes, an incongruity which fascinated Major Trommel. Her great full breasts lolled sideways under her nightdress against the pillow, and the curve of her hip made an opulent alp beneath the sheet.

'I hope it is real coffee and not that filth made of acorns,' she said, and then: 'You *have* a fat little pot for such a thin little man, haven't you? I had not noticed before.'

Major Trommel drew in his belly quickly and said with hauteur, 'I have not of late enjoyed the exercise to which I am accustomed,' then snatched his trousers from where they lay neatly folded on a chair.

'Really?' the Countess said significantly. 'Exercise is the last thing you have been short of, I should have thought. Perhaps it is the wrong kind: you never seem to get any-where very much, do you?'

Major Trommel snarled as he hopped on the floor with one leg in his trousers; the Countess smiled sweetly and lay back while he dressed. She regarded the ceiling where a fat Virgin and an even fatter Child flew across a heaven of bolster-shaped clouds on which sat an assortment of winged but obese and aerodynamically dubious *putti*, and after a few moments she asked, 'Have you done anything yet about the oil?'

Trommel thrust the tail of his shirt into his trousers and tightened the belt viciously.

'Oil!' he said. 'What do I care about your stupid oil?'

He sniffed and went to the other window at the opposite end of the vast bedroom, looking down over the roofs of the village: he could just see part of the eastern end of the parapet with a hundred-foot drop beyond. Now that the sun was higher the plain was a distant haze, all the way to the front line. By day it chattered and thumped invisibly, but at night the chattering and thumping were accompanied by far-off flickers of light. *Ach Gott*, he thought, this accursed pigeon-chest, but for which I could die like a hero.

'My poor unit,' he said. 'Gone, vanished utterly, save for myself and the faithful Wohlhaber. Disappeared into the *Ewigkeit*.'

He drew a hand over his eyes and fastened his uniform collar.

The Countess sat up in bed with her hands clasped round her knees, gazing darkly at them, and said, 'If my Federico were alive he would see about the oil. My Federico was a proper soldier.' She sniffed. '*Ahimè*! His bones lie in glory on the field of Harar.'

'Staunchly facing the Italian lines with forty Ethiopian spears in his backside, no doubt,' said the major tartly. 'Don't tell me. I personally witnessed the irresistible advance of Marshal Graziani's armies into the British prison camps in the Western Desert.'

'Poltroon! Analphabetic!' the Countess screamed. 'And what of you? You have been advancing backwards for four years, and yet you insult the memory of my noble husband after you have shared my bed on several arid occasions! If you think you can even begin to compare with him on any point at all . . . !'

Major Trommel went to the cheval-glass and checked his collar, then turned and said offhandedly, 'Of course I apologise, if that is the way you take it. Hrrm, it is true that I have had some slight disability of late—hrrmf, purely temporary, I assure you.' Or is it? he thought with horror. Am I getting old? He went to the bed and patted the auburn hair with caution, as though it might burn him. The Countess flinched away and he said reassuringly, 'I'll think about the oil, my dear. Now please say you are no longer angry with me, eh?'

'Very well,' she said pouting.

Trommel caressed her cheek; she twisted her head and bit his hand, yelling with laughter as he danced about shaking and sucking it. The door opened and Wohlhaber appeared on the threshold. He held a tray of coffee things and stood rigid with the tray quite motionless. He was fully dressed, and his face and boots shone, the face as expressionless as the boots while Major Trommel capered unaware until the Countess pointed over his shoulder. Turning, still sucking his hand, Trommel saw Wohlhaber and stamped his foot.

'Come in, dolt!' he yapped, then turned brusquely to the Countess. 'Your coffee. I shall not remain. I have my duties. Wohlhaber shall bring my coffee to the command post.'

He strode out, slamming the door.

The Countess gazed pensively at Wohlhaber, then got out of bed and stretched in the thin nightgown; the muscles of Wohlhaber's jaws stood out like walnuts as she came closer to him and he inhaled her perfume. Then she smiled at him and the tray trembled, cups dancing on their saucers. She ran a finger round the line of his chin, purred, 'Poor simple soldier, so far from home,' and began to unbutton his uniform.

Eventually she moved back from Wohlhaber and said, 'Still at attention? You may put down the tray.'

Wohlhaber obeyed, swallowing, and the Countess twined her arms round his neck, leaning heavily on him while he gulped and swayed. At last the Countess murmured, 'You recall Major Trommel's commands to you when you were at the fountain?'

In a strangled voice Wohlhaber said, 'Word for word, *gnädige Frau Gräfin*.'

'Good.'

She led him to the bed and softly said, 'One'; and by the time she had reached 'Three' the coffee was quite cold.

2

AND in another square, much farther south, Major William Widdicombe was shaving in a mirror attached to a stanchion of the three-tonner while Sergeant-Cook Entwistle supervised the preparation of breakfast by Corporal-Cook White and Private Dorbell, in turn supervised by numerous locals.

The locals said, 'Poor Italy, poor us, the Germans have stolen everything away. Cigarettes? Chocolates? Soap?' and Corporal White said to Private Dorbell, 'Watch it, Knocker, not so much bleeding fat in that pan and for Jeeeesus' sake turn the bleeding heat down, it's supposed to be an omelet not a bleeding cremation,' and Private Dorbell said, 'All I can say is roll on that boat,' and Sergeant Entwistle said, 'Hark at 'im, Blacky! Get yer bloody knees brown, Dorbell, and when am I gointer get me bloody shai?'

Major Widdicombe scraped away the last of the lather, observed the reflection of his round white face and thought, You handsome beast!

The water in the brew-tin boiled. Dorbell threw in a handful of tea and waited a moment before adding the condensed milk and the sugar. Major Widdicombe turned, resplendent in new khaki drill bush-jacket and shorts, fawn stockings and brown brogues, just as Sergeant Entwistle said, 'Shai up, sir,' presenting him with a dripping mug.

Widdicombe took it and said irritably, 'Shai, shai. Speak English, Sergeant, for God's sake. You're not in Egypt now.'

'Yessir,' Entwistle said. 'Tea.' He sipped and said reflectively, 'Dorbell's learning. Proper kwais ketir, this shai, I mean tea.'

Major Widdicombe cursed the fate that had landed him with Entwistle, White and Dorbell. They were all four of them replacements for Main H.Q. Eighth Army: Major Widdicombe and Private Dorbell straight out from England; Entwistle and White from Caserta, which they had reached via Egypt, North Africa, Sicily and Anzio, well to the rear but regarding themselves as seasoned veterans. They wore their stripes of rank Eighth Army fashion, on the right sleeve only, not sewn on but held in place by strips of A.T.S. issue knicker elastic, souvenirs of an historic action during a joint visit to the Pyramids.

The major sat apart to eat his breakfast in the shadow of the truck, the officer's mess. Entwistle squatted on the sunny side, the sergeants' mess. White and Dorbell ate standing together, and the Italians watched the segregated meal with interest.

Corporal White for his part was watching the Italians, and he said to Dorbell, 'Hey, Knocker, have a shufti at that bint in the green frock.'

Dorbell said aggrievedly, 'I wish you'd talk English, Corp. I dunno no Eyetie.' On a wall behind White was written *Italiani! Non vendete le vostre figlie per una scatoletta di carne!* among other graffiti. Dorbell said, 'What's it say on that wall then, Corp?'

White turned and glanced at the wall.

'It says Viva Mussolini but then they've crossed out Mussolini and put in Churchill, and then it says D.D.T.

1943, and then it says Don't flog yer daughters fer a tinner bully.' He looked again at the girl in the green frock. 'If I'd seen her last night I'd have given her *two* tins.'

Through a rasher of bacon Dorbell said, 'That's promiscuss, that is. You ought to feel condemned. Why, when I joined the Army eight years ago . . .'

'Eight years? You've not been in the army five minutes yet.'

'Not this army,' Dorbell said patiently. '*The* Army. The Salvation Army I'm talking about, like when I got saved in 1937 I felt condemned before, if you see what I mean. You never been saved, Corp?'

Corporal White said, 'No bleeding fear I ain't and I'm not going to, not by you. Not till you've put three stripes up and made it an order, and that day'll come when they make Fizzer Bert Entwistle a full general.'

Sergeant Entwhistle was sweating in the hot sunshine, helped by his bacon and egg and pint of scalding tea. He thought, By God, officers got it cushy, noshing bloody omelet in the shade, him and his flaming speak English. . . . Wait a minute now, Fitzherbert, stan'esh shwaieh; and got up from his bedroll, moving round the three-tonner into the shade, standing to attention and coughing.

'What is it, Sergeant?'

Entwistle feigned embarrassment.

'Well, sir, I don't know how to put it . . .'

'Come on, man!'

Sergeant Entwistle said, 'Well, sir, you might take offence.'

'Nonsense,' Widdicombe said. 'I want you to tell me what's on your mind. You can speak man to man.'

'Right you are, sir,' the sergeant said happily. 'It's your knees.'

Major Widdicombe regarded them, pallid unbaked loaves.

'What about 'em?'

Sergeant Entwistle coughed again and said, 'Well, sir, you ought to get them a bit sunburned before we reach Main H.Q. The officers who've been out here some time'll make jokes about not having got your knees brown.'

The major flushed and said coldly, 'I see. Thank you for telling me, Sergeant. We will change places.'

'Yessir,' said Entwistle, and yelled for Dorbell to make the transfer. Major Widdicombe sat with his knees to the sun, sweating, and while White and Dorbell struck camp, Sergeant Entwistle dozed in the shade of the truck, content.

Major Widdicombe thought, Good chap that Entwistle, just as long as he doesn't give himself any airs. But I need some suntan oil. Is there a N.A.A.F.I.? Might send Dorbell in to buy some. Or an officer's shop? He looked round at the single street of devastated or newly repaired buildings and decided there probably wasn't. Oil. Olive oil would do. What the hell was oil in Italian? He pulled out a pocket dictionary and riffled through the pages. Oil. *Olio*. Sun. *Sole*. He thrust the dictionary back into the side pocket of his bush-jacket, stood up and went to the small knot of Italians, selecting an old man huddled in a long black cloak next to the girl in the green frock. The old man regarded him with lizard eyes. Major Widdicombe raised a knee and pointed to it.

'*Sole*,' he said, and then made a vague gesture at the buildings behind. '*Olio*.'

The girl in the green frock said dispassionately and at large, 'Another madman,' and to Widdicombe: 'Hey, madman, thy dirty buttocks are even bigger than thy fat knees.'

Corporal White said, 'Stone me, Knocker, I do believe he's getting off with her.'

Major Widdicombe smiled politely at the girl and asked, 'Do you speak English?' He raised his voice and repeated slowly, the words spaced out, 'Do . . . you . . . speak . . . English?'

The girl smiled back, nodded and said, 'Fackandblindyou costa feefty Locky Stryeek.'

Major Widdicombe flushed and turned back to the old man, shouting, 'Have you any oil? Oilio, I mean *olio* for the *sole*, damn it all?'

The old man sighed and said in a strong American accent, 'Why'n hell you keep hollerin' like that? Ain't no oil up here; ain't none till you get way south, mebbe far as Bari. Down there they got oil. Whyn't you just cover up them goddam ugly knees?'

Private Dorbell said lugubriously, 'Striking a bargain with her dad I bet he's doing, Corp. Soomwhere over them hills is the Scarlet Woman of Rorm, O Lord deliver us and save the major.'

Widdicombe clicked his tongue and left the Italians, going to the cooking stove. He said to Corporal White, 'Give me some butter for my knees, Corporal.'

Private Dorbell said, 'The power of prayer has to be seen to be believed, sir.'

'Who's talking about prayer? I want to butter my knees. Now come on, Corporal.'

'Yessir, butter your knees, sir,' said Corporal White impassively. 'I'll get the butter now, sir.'

*   *   *

They rolled north in the endless military traffic of the coast road, then stopped at Fano for lunch, sitting on the little stone mole and looking out over the Adriatic.

16

'Are we going to rest here for a bit, sir?' Sergeant Entwistle asked, gazing at the water.

'We'll take an hour,' Widdicombe said. 'Get a spot more sunshine on these knees.'

'Very good, sir.'

Entwistle got up and went to the truck, returning a few moments later with a fishing rod.

'Fishing?' Widdicombe said. 'Didn't know you were a fisherman, Sergeant.'

Entwistle nodded, fitting a reel to the rod and threading line through the rings. He tied on a length of gut, sliding a float up it, then a hook.

'Bait,' he said, rubbing his chin with one hand and staring into a little open box. 'Try one of these. Artificial maggot.'

The other watched, White nudging Dorbell with amusement as the sergeant cast out from the stonework on which he stood, allowing the bait to drift along on the small waves. Their amusement changed to interest as the float swirled under the surface, the rod bent, and Entwistle was playing a fish. As he landed it they gathered round, seeing an elongated, needle-nosed creature about sixteen inches long. It flapped and wriggled until Entwistle dispatched it.

'Good God,' said Widdicombe. 'What is it—a baby swordfish?'

'Garfish,' Entwistle said. 'Very good eating. The water's full of 'em.'

He caught six more, all on the same artificial maggot.

'Funny,' he said as he packed away his tackle. 'Got green bones, these fellers have. We'll nosh 'em for supper to-night.'

Soon afterwards they pushed on. Sergeant Entwistle drove with the Major next to him; White and Dorbell sat on their kit in the back of the truck. Held up in Rimini by the traffic, they gazed in awe at the armoured vehicles in the huge tank repair depot. Major Widdicombe felt his eyes smarting with pride: he was a part of Eighth Army, the army of Alamein and late of Montgomery!

As they continued, signs proliferated at the roadside. Private Dorbell stood up and read three signs in succession: *Wasky Most*, *Wyrwa*, *Spital Wojenny*, the last one adorned by the figure of a mermaid holding sword and shield, emblem of the Polish Corps. He sat down and said, 'Ee, it's a foony lingo, is Eyetie. Wasky most, whirrwah, spittle woe-jenny. I'll remember it even if I dunno what it means. You never know, Corp, it might come in handy.'

Major Widdicombe chose the night halt with care, not far from the church of San Vitale at Classe, near Ravenna— he had been told he ought to see the mosaics if ever he got the chance—and picked a marsh with a thousand shellholes in it. He trudged off towards the church, leaving the others to make camp and supper, gazed at the mosaics thinking, Stiff-looking lot, wonder why they crack 'em up so much, fiddling job sticking all those little bits and pieces together; and left the church, returning along the path skirting the shellholes. Halfway back to the camp he halted, staring down at a thin soldier in denims who was kneeling on the path, digging carefully. Major Widdicombe coughed; the soldier flicked a glance upward, then went back to his task.

Widdicombe quacked with outrage.

'Stand to attention and salute!' he said.

'In a minute,' the soldier said wearily, and unearthed an object like a large, thick discus with a nut on the top centre. He took out a spanner and worked on the nut.

'What's that?' said Widdicombe. 'And why don't you obey my order? What the hell are you up to?'

The soldier said, 'It's a mine. Detector party's up along there. They find 'em, I fix 'em.'

'A mine? You mean—an explosive mine?'

'Well, it isn't a coalmine, is it? There's near on a hundred thousand uncleared mines round about here.'

Widdicombe stood transfixed while the soldier took the top off the mine, fiddled briefly, said, 'Another one for the pot,' and threw the mine into a shellhole. 'I'll salute you now if you want.'

'Don't bother,' said Widdicombe. 'Just get up and walk *in front of me* to that three-tonner over there.'

The soldier scrambled to his feet, turned and walked away, Major Widdicombe following at some distance and placing his feet exactly in the soldier's footprints, sweat rolling down his face. At the truck he said, 'You may dismiss,' and flopped into a seat as the soldier walked away whistling.

'Have an interesting shufti round, sir?' Sergeant Entwistle asked.

*   *   *

After a night spent listening to the racket of a million frogs and the dynamo whine of countless mosquitoes, the party crawled from beneath their nets at dawn, broke camp hurriedly after a cold breakfast, and filled up at the nearest petrol point. On the road again, Major Widdicombe inspected his knees and was disappointed. They had turned faintly pink, but that was all. Certainly he would never get his knees brown sitting in the cab of a three-ton truck. He dozed for an hour and a half, then jumped into wakefulness as a huge American truck overtook the three-tonner with a roar, G.I.s jeering from the back. The American truck disappeared round a curve in the road, while behind the three-tonner a dispatch-rider stopped his motor-cycle and sneezed in the dust-cloud.

They saw the sign round the curve: the Crusader cross on

the shield and the legend 8th ARMY MAIN pointing up the little side road. Entwistle swung the wheel round and followed the signpost; the three-tonner ground out of sight as the dispatch-rider reached the sign, which the American truck had touched in passing. He stopped again, said, 'Them bloody Yanks,' and restored the sign to its correct position, pointing up the main road.

*   *   *

Major Trommel awoke in the command post, thinking that he had better get on with the day's routine. Half past five, and nothing done. From a back room of the converted house a generator chugged quietly. Trommel glanced round the whitewashed walls, yawning, then rose from his desk and went over to the battered old Tornister 'B' radio. He sat down at the operator's desk and sighed, switching on the transmitter and listening to the increasing hum as it warmed up. He put on the headphones, depressed the key a few times, then switched on the receiver hopefully. Nothing. But the units of the Wehrmacht changed their operating frequencies and unit callsigns every night, punctually at midnight. By now Trommel had no idea what his callsign was, what frequency he should be sending on; and anyway he knew no morse. But duty was duty. The strength report first. He laid down the headphones and went back to his own desk, picking up the block of forms.

> *Officers.* 1
> *N.C.O.s.* Nil
> *Other Ranks.* 1
> *Killed.* ?
> *Wounded.* ?
> *Missing.* 12

Trommel spiked the form on top of a thick wad of un-sent out-going messages on the operator's desk. Above the radio equipment a notice read *Der Feind hört mit*. Trommel thought, Well, if the enemy are listening, they'll hear the same as the Hauptquartier of the German XIV Army. Static electricity. He returned and picked up the ammuni-tion-state report, filling it in carefully by copying it from the previous day's, which was the same as that of the day before. Indeed, no ammunition had been used for six weeks, ever since Wohlhaber had shot a mad dog at the urgent request of an agitated peasant. The dog had been writhing about on a sofa in the best room, foaming at the mouth, and the peasant had yelled, 'Shoot it, shoot it!' So Wohlhaber had shot it, and the sofa, and a large china vase standing in a corner behind the sofa, demonstrating very effectively his own limitations and the carrying power of 9 mm. parabellum.

The situation report. Trommel yawned again and scribbled the standard phrases: 'Situation quiet . . . continual artillery and anti-aircraft fire audible to north-eastward . . . nothing new to report.' He initialled the form, spiked it, sighed. Surely Headquarters would send a message for him soon; even have him relieved? A dispatch-rider would come, a staff car, even? He sighed again, yawned again. Wohlhaber would be coming over any moment now, having finished helping with the domestic work at the palazzo. Popular fellow with the women, Wohlhaber: he got on tremendously with the cook and the maid. Best type of Teutonic manhood—or would have been if he'd had a bit more upstairs. Wohlhaber's body and my brains, Trommel mused. If I had been stronger, with a good broad chest like Wohlhaber's, why, I might have had an Iron Cross to sport on it. Deeds of valour and so forth, a kiss on both cheeks from the Führer. . . .

Trommel frowned, wondering about the impact of that scrubby little toothbrush moustache, when the door opened and Wohlhaber stood in the entrance, saluting meticulously. Major Trommel heard the roar of a motor increasing in the distance. The staff car! He leaped to his feet.

'Sir, beg to report there's a truck coming up the road.' Wohlhaber glanced over his shoulder. 'It's in the square now.'

Major Trommel beamed.

Wohlhaber said, 'Excuse me, sir, but you look pleased.'

'Pleased? Of course I am pleased, you great sack. But why should they send a truck? I am a major, and I have the right to a staff car.'

Wohlhaber said, 'Perhaps the English don't know about that, sir.'

'The English?'

Wohlhaber jerked a thumb over his shoulder as Major Trommel ran to the doorway, peered past Wohlhaber, blenched, then scurried back to a machine-gun embrasure, wrenching at the gun, which had been fixed with great forethought so that it could command a section of road below. The barrel clanked on the side of the concrete slit, needing another hundred degrees of traverse. Trommel gave up the effort, turned, grabbing at the Lüger in its holster, drew the pistol as a round white face appeared behind Wohlhaber. Trommel aimed at the face and pulled the trigger, which clicked.

'Damnation,' said Trommel, his teeth chattering as he retreated behind his desk, remembering that he had emptied the gun six weeks before in order to count the rounds of ammunition in the magazine.

'What the hell are you playing at?' the newcomer said in English, pushing past Wohlhaber with curiosity, looking

22

round the command post and then at the strange uniforms. 'I'm looking for Main H.Q. Eighth Army. Who are you lot, Polish or what?' His eyes rested on an old copy of the *Völkischer Beobachter* with a headline in Gothic script which read 'Eastern Front: Heroic Resistance—the Führer's speech.'

'Good God,' he said. 'That's German. You're Germans, by God.'

He fiddled with the press-button flap of his holster and yanked out his officer-issue .38 Smith and Wesson revolver, jerking it up into the aim: the ill-adjusted lanyard round his neck tightened and caused the pressure of his finger to pull the trigger. The gun went off with a tremendous roar, the bullet striking one of the walls at an angle, all three men flinging themselves to the floor until the *whangg-whangg* of the ricochets ceased. Major Widdicombe slipped on the safety-catch surreptitiously and stood up.

'Now then,' he said. 'Get up and stand over there.'

He gestured with the pistol. Trommel and Wohlhaber ranged themselves obediently in front of the radio desk.

Trommel pointed sadly to the radio and said in slow, careful English, 'That is where your bullet finally landed. You have broken the wireless.'

Three more men appeared behind the British officer, who said, 'Jerries! I've captured some Jerries!' Then he looked at Major Trommel and said, 'Now suppose you tell me who you are.'

The major clicked his heels, bowed and said, 'Trommel.'

Major Widdicombe swallowed and thought, Christ, just for a moment I thought he said Rommel. But the luck of it, the sheer heaven-sent luck! I'll get a Military Cross or something pinned on me for this, by the King!

Major Trommel said, 'This is Private Wohlhaber.'

Widdicombe was about to say, 'How do you do,' but

recollected himself. He said instead, 'You are my prisoners.' A cackle of glee escaped him. Half a minute in the country and he'd taken some prisoners! Two, anyhow.

The German officer bowed again, a tear trickling from his left eye; he sniffed and wiped away the tear with the back of his hand, then passed over the Lüger butt foremost. Major Widdicombe accepted it, suddenly unsure of himself. What the devil did one do next?

Major Trommel said, 'In the circumstances, I should be willing to offer parole on behalf of myself and this soldier.'

'Oh, yes,' said Major Widdicombe with relief. 'Yes of course, parole. Good idea, that. But don't you try any monkey business.' He was beginning to enjoy himself, and added fiercely, 'Or I'll blast you.'

He gestured once more with the pistol, and his two captives moved out of the command post, Widdicombe following.

Private Dorbell said, 'He's got two Jerries.'

'*We've* got two Jerries,' Corporal White corrected him. 'Part of his unit, aren't we? There you are, then.'

Private Dorbell said, 'Ee, I do feel proud.'

Sergeant Entwistle was shouting, 'Yalla, imshi, inn' al kus oumak!' at a small knot of villagers which had materialised. They were saying, 'English. Without doubt he is speaking English. We are liberated,' and they raised a cheer. A fat woman in black shoved forward a very little girl holding a bunch of artificial flowers; she bobbed a curtsey and presented them to Major Widdicombe, who clutched the flowers in one hand and his gun in the other. A few people clapped; Widdicombe started to escort his prisoners to the truck; and then a screech of paralysing intensity halted him instantly. There was a sudden hush, and Widdicombe saw a statuesque woman wearing a salmon-pink dress and carrying a mauve parasol open above her Titian head. She was standing majestically at the opposite side of the square.

'Fine figure of a woman, that,' Widdicombe said. 'Cut above this lot too: wonder who she is?'

The woman was yelling and beckoning; British and Germans drifted across the square as though compelled by some cacophonous Lorelei.

'That is the Countess of San Marco,' Major Trommel said. 'She is, as it were, the civil power now.'

When they reached the Countess she shouted at Major Widdicombe in Italian, 'Never-educated imbecile! How dare you liberate my village without asking my permission?'

Major Widdicombe said, 'Good afternoon, madam. Er . . .' He turned to his men and said, 'Any of you speak Italian?'

Sergeant Entwistle was about to speak, but Dorbell forestalled him.

'A bit, sir,' he said.

'Come on then,' Widdicombe said testily.

Private Dorbell moved in front of the Countess and gazed at her, peering up past the pink cliffs of her breasts. He said, 'Whirrwah. Um—spittle woe-jenny?'

The Countess said in amazement, 'What is this? Are you after all some kind of *slavi*: Serbs or something?'

Private Dorbell said, 'Wasky most.'

'What's all that about?' Major Widdicombe asked.

'I dunno what it means, sir,' Private Dorbell told him. 'I just read it on some notices.'

'Get out of the way, you fool.'

Widdicombe turned to Major Trommel, who had been standing correctly at ease, a faint smile on his face.

'Look,' he said, 'what about you? Can you tell her who we are and so forth?'

Major Trommel said coldly, 'Under the terms of the Geneva Convention I am not compelled to assist the enemy. My duty is to give you my name, rank, and serial number —and that is all.' He added the translation in German to Private Wohlhaber, who sprang to attention and nodded.

Sergeant Entwistle said, 'I speak a bit of Eyetie, sir, but I tell you what. Let me have five minutes with me meat cleaver at the bastard.'

'No, no,' Trommel protested in haste. 'That will not be necessary. Private Wohlhaber will now be able to testify that I am acting under duress.' He turned to the Countess and said, 'This swine is a British officer and I suppose these are his men. At all events they have taken me prisoner, not to mention poor Wohlhaber.'

The Countess said sweetly to Widdicombe in English, 'My dear Major, welcome to Borgo San Marco,' and Major Trommel subsided speechless.

'Well, I really think you might have spared us all that,' Widdicombe told her. 'However, my name is Widdicombe—Major William Widdicombe.' He pointed in turn: 'Sergeant Entwistle, Corporal White, Private Dorbell.'

The Countess acknowledged their existence with a regal wave of the hand.

'What brave soldiers,' she said, and Trommel scowled.

Widdicombe said, 'Cooks. They are all cooks.'

The Countess looked a little taken aback at first, and then her eyes gleamed.

'Cooks? Oh, but that is wonderful! Doubtless you have food? And perhaps oil?'

'Bags of food. And a cooker,' said Widdicombe. 'But it's a funny thing, that. We've no oil. I was looking for some yesterday for, um, well something. Couldn't find any, though.'

'We will talk about it later,' said the Countess. 'You will be my guests at the palazzo. Come, gentlemen,' and she gave Major Widdicombe her arm. Trommel sneered as the Englishman juggled with the pistol and the artificial flowers, finally handing the flowers to Sergeant Entwistle, who brought up the rear glumly.

'I bet she's a real hooer of Babylon,' Private Dorbell said.

'I hope so,' said Sergeant Entwistle. 'Now cop hold of these flowers while I go and fetch the truck.'

3

THEY had chicken soup, then the garfish transmuted by Entwistle and White into *orphie pompadour*, served with tartare sauce; they had no means of making potato croquettes, so used crisp fettucine, and plenty of them. The Countess and Major Trommel devoured the garfish.

'I have not tasted fresh fish for two years,' the Countess said, delighted. Trommel did not speak: his mouth was too full.

Widdicombe grunted, dissecting his fish and inspecting the translucent green bones doubtfully. But when he tasted the fish he found it very good indeed, if rather oily. They finished the meal with a huge steamed treacle pudding. Earlier Widdicombe had taken Sergeant Entwistle aside and told him, 'Finish off with something filling. I've got a hunch there isn't too much food about in this place.' Now he himself could eat no more, but the Countess and Major Trommel ate about a pound and a half of pudding each. Then at last the Countess sighed like a collapsing dirigible, wiping her mouth with her napkin.

'Ah,' she said. 'What a meal! Major Widdicombe, you and your men must stay here at the palazzo until the war is finished. Is it too much to ask you to agree, Major Trommel?'

'It was an excellent meal, certainly,' Trommel said grudgingly. 'I could not go so far as that, though. Do not think me ungrateful, but it is a pity we had no wine, not even a sip of cognac to follow.'

Major Widdicombe looked over the gloomy mahogany table, laid with silver plate and cut crystal glinting in the light of a single naked electric bulb which was fed by the generator at the command post. The highlights in the Countess's hair were beautiful, he thought. Indeed, she was a beautiful woman in every respect, if a little too generous.

He said, 'Do you mean there is nothing to drink in the village?'

'Nothing. It is a desert. We have not had a drop of wine —and more important, not a drop of oil. The oil, you understand . . .'

She broke off as Widdicombe rose with a muttered apology and went to the doors, opening them and going some way along the hall, calling for Corporal White.

White was sitting on a rush-bottomed chair in the huge tiled kitchen with Filomena the housemaid, Gina the cook, and Sergeant Entwistle. The artificial flowers huddled mustily in a fat terra cotta vase on the scrubbed kitchen table: Filomena was sniffing at them absently, waiting for Corporal White's next move. She was sixteen, with hair the colour of a blackbird's wing, sleek and smooth, while Gina was perhaps ten years older, with a black frizz of hair and fat red lips. White was edging his chair closer to Filomena's when he heard Major Widdicombe's shout. He sighed, got up resignedly and left the kitchen, returning almost immediately.

'A bottle of gin and a bottle of Scotch,' he said. 'Proper night of it they're going to make. I dunno, it seems all wrong to me, him sitting there with that Jerry, not to speak of that other 'un waiting at table. I mean to say we're bleeding *enemies* aren't we?'

Sergeant Entwistle laid his hand more firmly on Gina's knee and said, 'How many times before you learn, Blacky? They're officers, him and that Jerry. Now you go and fetch his flipping booze or you'll find yourself on a fizzer.'

Corporal White departed, and Filomena said to Gina in dialect, 'He is beautiful, isn't he?'

Gina said, 'Yes, but this one is strong. I have not seen a strong man for years except for the German servant.'

'You saw enough of him.'

'And so did you. You in the morning, me in the evening.'

Filomena gasped, a hand at her mouth.

'Gina, you knew about me?'

'Fool, of course I knew.' She grinned and reached across to pat Filomena's hand. 'I taught him, then he taught you. And now he is teaching the Countess.'

Filomena giggled, and Gina went on, 'Not that *she* has anything to learn.'

They collapsed, and Sergeant Entwistle said, 'Hey, what's the joke then?'

*　　　　*　　　　*

Wohlhaber was clearing away the coffee things, and the Countess was saying to Major Widdicombe, 'Yes, the first mayor was a fascist. But they shot him, and then the second mayor was appointed: a communist partisan. The other partisan groups did not care for this, so they shot the communist. Then two more partisan leaders wanted to be mayor, so they fought a duel in the square with revolvers; very Far West.'

'You mean Wild West,' Widdicombe said. 'What happened?'

Major Trommel said succinctly, 'They shot each other. Now there is no mayor.'

'And that is why I am the civil authority,' said the Countess. 'And why I want to talk to you about the oil.'

Just then Corporal White burst into the room with a bottle of gin in one hand and a bottle of whisky in the other.

'Damn it all,' Major Widdicombe said. 'I know I told you to hurry up, but that's taking things too far. You might at least remember to knock.'

'It's the three-tonner, sir,' White gasped. 'It's gone!'

'Gone?'

'Well, most of it, sir. Come and see.'

White put down the bottles on the table, and the whole party left, except for Wohlhaber, who had taken a tray or crockery to the kitchen. They trooped out into the street through the arch of the carriage-gates to where the truck had stood. They could still see the chassis in the gloom, a stark skeleton of greasy steel, but everything else had vanished: body, engine, running gear and electrical system. The Countess began to shriek histrionically in Italian, at the same time appearing to extract a good deal of amusement from the situation.

'Good job we off-loaded the cooker and the stores and such,' Entwistle said.

Trommel said in a detached manner, 'Just what I would have expected. It is the same all over the country. Leave a vehicle unattended and they will strip it down in five minutes. You should have left a guard on it.'

'But I did,' Major Widdicombe protested. 'Corporal, where the devil is Dorbell? Oh lord, there'll be the hell to pay over this.' He bellowed, 'Dorbell! Dorbell, where are you?'

'I'm here, sir,' said a hollow voice behind him, and they

turned to see Dorbell's dim figure coming across the courtyard buttoning his braces; tucked under his arm was a copy of the *Berliner Neue Zeitung* with a couple of pages missing. The Countess began to laugh.

'Dorbell, where have you been, man?'

Dorbell said with an abashed glance at the Countess, 'I've been to be excused, sir. The German officer's batman was in the kitchen, dodging in and out with dirty dishes, and he lent me this paper. Ee, summat's happened to the trook!'

Major Trommel frowned.

'We had better return to the dining room and interview Wohlhaber,' he suggested.

'Damned good idea,' said Widdicombe.

On the way he asked White, 'Tell me, Corporal, what d'you think'll happen? About the truck, I mean.'

'You'll be court-martialled, sir,' White said cheerfully. 'I knew a case just like it when I was at Tel el Kebir— three-tonner like this, too. They didn't put the officer in the nick or anything, just stopped his pay. One of them big Bedfords cosses nearly two thousand quid.'

'Oh my God, Corporal. Are you telling the truth?'

'God's honour, sir,' White said briskly. 'He was a D. of E. officer just like you, so he had to sign on for another five years to get the repayments in.'

Major Widdicombe tottered into the dining room and sat down, White leaving him at the door. The Countess came next, dabbing with a monogrammed cambric handkerchief at the laughter-tears in her eyes. Trommel entered, saw the bottles on the table and said politely to Widdicombe, 'Well, Major, do you mind if I—er, do the honourables?'

Widdicombe made a hopeless gesture with a hand like a seal's flipper; Trommel bowed and poured drinks, sipped, sighed with deep solace.

'*Ausgezeichnet!*' he smiled. 'Major, your Scotch whisky almost compensates me for the fate which has befallen me. Now, Wohlhaber.'

He strode to the door and yelled for his servant, gulped the whisky and poured himself another glass, sipping until Wohlhaber appeared.

Major Trommel quacked at his servant while Widdicombe abstracted himself, understanding nothing and thinking, Oh God, what have I done? A court-martial! Two thousand pounds! Disgrace! If I were a man I'd go and cut my throat. Then he brightened. He drained his glass and thought, There's a way. I'll *march* these bloody Jerries to Main H.Q., that's what I'll do. Say the truck was a write-off because of enemy action, that's it! I know, a mine like that one I saw the other day: no, yesterday it was; bloody hell, it all seems a month ago. But if I *march* 'em in—heroic action against odds—heavy enemy fire—gallant resistance —two prisoners—heh-heh, we're home and dry. But what about the others? Easy—tell 'em I'll recommend them all for a gong.

He suddenly realised that Major Trommel was speaking to him.

'Eh?'

'My servant denies any complicity in the matter, Major. He deposes that he was outside the kitchen when the private solder under your command indicated that he had —hrrm, an urgent personal matter to attend to, and requested paper. By signs, you understand. He gave him paper and that was the end of it. This he assures me on his word of honour as a German soldier, and I believe him.'

'Oh, very well,' Widdicombe said. 'You can let him go.'

The Countess said, 'Oh, what a pity. I love to see him standing to attention.'

Wohlhaber kept his hands rigid, palms open at his sides, pressed against the wads of five-thousand-lira notes which filled his trouser pockets; he was thinking how very much better this was than the Russian front. Soon a nice polite British prison camp, perhaps even a spell in England working on a farm. Lovely. Nine hundred and fifty thousand lire he'd got; those Italian crooks had swindled him of course, but still it would do. Have to hide it somewhere and then come back for it after the war.

'You may go, Wohlhaber,' said Major Trommel.

Wohlhaber saluted and was gone.

Major Widdicombe got up holding the gin bottle and went jauntily over to the Countess saying, 'My dear lady! All that soldiers' talk, and we have been neglecting you. Pray permit me,' and he sloshed a large measure of neat gin into her glass: she simpered as he lifted his own to her, and they clinked glasses.

'Here's to a bloody war, and perdition to the enemy,' Widdicombe said, carried away by his new rollicking mood; then he remembered Major Trommel and said to him, 'Oh, sorry. No offence, old man.'

Trommel bowed stiffly, thinking, These English are just as insane as one has been led to believe. The swine was ready to weep into his whisky five minutes ago, and now look at him!

The Countess sipped her gin, looking at Widdicombe and thinking, He is fat, but looks as if he has a strong back. Federico was shaped rather similarly, sort of pear-fashion and steatopygous. Does that connote amorous propensities, appropriate musculature? We shall see, possibly.

'Ah well,' Major Widdicombe said, stretching and yawning. 'Been a long day: I think I'll turn in.' He looked at Trommel with what he hoped was a suitably martial expression and said, 'I know you're on parole, but just remember one of my men will be awake all night—and armed. Orders to shoot on sight.'

*   *   *

He awoke some time before dawn, and as his senses returned he found two hot arms round his waist and a hot, snoring breath at the back of his neck. In the confusion of wakening, Major Widdicombe assumed that he was being attacked, that his assailant's next move would be to bury a knife in his back, and he hurtled out of bed with a strangled squeak, hitting a rug with both feet. The rug skidded on the marble floor, which Major Widdicombe struck with the back of his head. Rubbing it and groaning, he staggered to his feet ready to run naked out of the palazzo, out of Borgo San Marco and straight for the British lines; and then he heard the lazy voice of the Countess asking whether he had hurt himself.

He whipped round, bent and picked up the rug, wrapping it with some difficulty about his waist. The room was very dim, but he could just discern her figure in the bed— his bed.

'Dreaming,' he stammered. 'I was dreaming. What— what are you doing in there?'

The Countess leaned back, and the major caught a glimpse in the half-light of two rosy, shadowed Kanchenjungas; he looked away hastily and then back again, groaning and rubbing his head with his free hand.

'Hurt my head,' he said, goggling. 'Damn it, I can't see a thing,' he said, staring and thinking, On my oath, what a woman! Never seen anything like those before in my born days.

'I had too much gin,' the Countess confessed. 'Too much gin. I must have come to the wrong room. Anyway, when

I woke up I was here.' She patted the bed. 'Come, sit down, Major.'

Mesmerised, he sat beside her.

'Bit unconventional, don't you think?' he said, and gave a hoarse cackle, her musky presence unnerving him.

She said, 'Ah, Major, war plays havoc with the conventions.' Then she sighed and said, 'Truly, you remind me of him.'

'Uh?'

'You remind me of my late husband. Poor Federico,' she said, sniffing and then beginning to cry in small sobs.

'Here, I say. There, there, then,' Major Widdicombe said, patting her shoulder; her sobs redoubled, so he put an arm round her and she buried her face on his chest. He felt a swinging Himalaya clump him on the side, and put out an uncertain hand, fear and caution giving way to elation as she stopped crying at once, gave a little gasp, grabbed the rug and tore it from him, hurling it away with a shriek. Major Widdicombe gripped the Countess by the shoulders and pushed her backwards: she gazed up at him with her huge eyes soft and melting, her wide mouth parted. Major Widdicombe prepared himself for the swoop, thinking, What a marvellous life! Two prisoners, and now an Italian *noblewoman*, and what's more after—how long?—must be a couple of months what with the troopship and everything, my God, Will Widdicombe launched again on the rolling seas of love.

He tensed his muscles for the leap into glory and oblivion, and the Countess said, 'Let me tell you about the oil first.'

'Oh no,' he groaned. 'Let it wait, please let it wait.'

The Countess frowned.

'First I will tell you about the oil. Afterwards, the transports of rapture.'

'Oh, hell,' he grumbled. 'Hurry up, though. This is murder.'

The Countess became brisk and businesslike. She sat up and said, 'Well then. The oil . . .'

From the open window came a sudden flash of light, then others, and a series of explosions trying to catch up the flashes. The major leaped out of bed and began to dress hurriedly.

'An attack!' he said. 'Where is it?'

He heard the roar of aircraft engines approaching fast, screaming overhead, followed a few seconds later by more explosions. The Countess sighed and joined him at the window.

'Down in the plain,' she said. 'They will not bother us here. Come back to bed and let me tell you about the oil.'

'Oh, bugger the oil,' Widdicombe shouted as he ran into the corridor fastening his bush-jacket.

'Beg your pardon, sir,' Sergeant Entwistle said as he emerged from a bedroom along the corridor, Gina's frizzy head peering round the door after him. 'There's a straff going on by the sound of it.'

'I know, you idiot. Where's Corporal White?'

The flashes and explosions continued. Major Widdicombe saw the next door open. Filomena appeared and scuttled away down the corridor, then White sauntered out and stiffened as he saw the major.

'I'll have something to say about this,' Widdicombe shouted.

'Yessir,' said Sergeant Entwistle with a significant stare past the major's shoulder. Widdicombe glanced behind him and saw the Countess coming forward like a breaking wave, in a froth of négligée. He slammed the door hastily in her face.

'Just been seeing if she was all right,' he said.

'Yessir,' said Sergeant Entwistle, deadpan.

'Well don't just stand there. Where's Dorbell?'

'Looking after the prisoners, sir.'

'God, that means they'll be halfway to Berlin by now. Come on, you two.'

They clattered downstairs to a small room opening off the kitchen. The electric lamp on its wandering lead had been transferred into this room, and by the faint light of the bulb and the brilliant glare of the intermittent flashes Major Trommel and Private Wohlhaber were trying to teach Dorbell the game of Skat. They were meeting resistance on two counts: Dorbell's conviction, tempered perforce by Major Trommel's rank, that card games were iniquitous; and Dorbell's natural lack of card-sense. He was scratching his head and saying resignedly, 'Oh well, then, what's troomps?' when Major Widdicombe came in, having left the sergeant and corporal outside.

'Pack that in,' he snapped at Dorbell.

Dorbell blew with relief and got to his feet.

'Dorbell, there's an attack going on.'

'Oh, is that what it is, sir?' said Dorbell with interest. 'I thought it was a thoonderstorm.'

'Go and make breakfast, you hear? Corporal White will stand guard. Then dress properly. Field service marching order. Breakfast at oh-six hundred hours.'

Major Trommel said politely, 'Forgive me, Major, but may I ask what you are going to do?'

'I'm going to take you up to Eighth Army right away,' Widdicombe said, and added dramatically, 'At oh-seven hundred hours, we march!'

4

'PRISONERS and escort, halt!'

At Major Widdicombe's order the small party shambled to a standstill, breathing heavily and wiping their brows, for even though it was early, they felt hot.

'If you want to wave, turn round and do it now,' said Major Widdicombe, gazing up to where three figures leaned over the distant parapet of the village square, high up and half a mile away. Widdicombe noticed that his feet were beginning to ache already.

'Last chance before we're out of sight,' he said.

They all waved, the British loosely from the elbow, the Germans stiffly, flapping rigid fingers against the palms of the hands, the three far-off figures of the Countess, Gina and Filomena making gestures similar to the Germans only with the hands turned inward—beckoning motions.

'Funny way them Eyeties got of waving,' said Corporal White. 'These Jerries and all.'

'Least they *are* waving,' Sergeant Entwistle said. ' 'Member when we marched out of Alex and they all said goodbye with chamberpots from the upstairs windows? Proper mush kwais that was.'

Major Widdicombe gave one last wave to the Countess,

straining his ears at a wailing cry which re-echoed among the barren faces of the hills.

'*O-o-o-oli-o-o-o!*'

Mad as a hatter. Widdicombe turned his back and led on down the road. Major Trommel and Private Wohl-haber came next, flanked by Entwistle and White at either side, Dorbell bringing up the rear and carrying Major Widdicombe's bedroll in addition to his own kit: he looked like a small snail with a large shell. They trudged round a bend in the road and Major Widdicombe looked back.

Out of sight. That's the last of that lot. And what a shower, he thought. Pity that woman's off her chump. Damned fine armful when you weigh it all up. Weigh it all up—rather good, that, must jot down these little jewels of wit someday. Shame missing those—what did she call it? Um, got it now, transports of rapture for God's sake: heard it called some funny things but that takes the old Peek Freans.

He tramped along, hearing the thud and creak and shuffle of the others' footsteps behind him. It was a superb day, the temperature climbing up through the seventies, the white road dazzling before him and obscured behind by a small cloud of dust which trailed the moving party. As they descended they passed cane-brakes dotted about near the roadside, then a few isolated patches of formerly cultivated ground where weeds throttled the untended vines, little clumps of beech and pine clustered in pockets of soil, and ever and again the green-black flames of the cypresses. There were no birds since they had all been slaughtered for food or sport. Major Widdicombe winced at a pain in his right heel.

They moved on for two hours, then sat by the roadside while Private Dorbell removed the brew-tin which hung from his large pack, gathered dry twigs and made a fire.

'Jolly good,' Major Widdicombe said as he watched. 'Must say I could do with a nice cup of tea.'

Major Trommel thought, The man is as mad as an Easter hare and as empty as a churn, and said, 'Are you quite sure you know where to take us?'

'Well, yes,' said Widdicombe. 'Yes: in a manner of speaking, that is. We'll trundle down to the main road and follow the signposts. I have a pretty shrewd idea they don't all point the right way, mind you. Still, we can ask; might even get a lift.'

'Follow the signposts!' Major Trommel said bitterly. 'Is that what you English soldiers do—follow signposts? I suppose you think you will follow signposts all the way to Berlin.'

'Don't be silly,' Major Widdicombe said. 'Of course we've got—er, maps and things. . . . Oh good, here comes the tea.'

They sat on the dusty grass and sipped in silence. Behind them Dorbell was hunched on Major Widdicombe's bedroll, Corporal White was passing a cigarette to Wohlhaber, and Sergeant Entwistle had vanished behind some bushes, taking his tea with him. Major Widdicombe pulled out his cigarette case and intercepted a greedy flicker from Major Trommel's eye. Widdicombe lighted a cigarette and puffed with exaggerated pleasure, leaving the case open at his side: there were eighteen cigarettes in full view of Major Trommel, who was now drumming his fingers on his knees and coughing from time to time in order to attract attention to himself. Major Widdicombe listened to the trickle of water, the stridulation of insects, and the occasional explosive cough from Trommel. Sarky old ramrod, him and his signposts, Widdicombe thought as he finished his tea. Let him suffer and serve him right.

The water caught Widdicombe's eye and reminded him of his aching feet. He rose and went over to the little stream, took off shoes and stockings and immersed his feet, gasping with relief and waggling his toes. Out of the corner of his eye he saw Major Trommel lean forward and pick up the cigarette case. Widdicombe thought, Right, you steal one of my fags and I'll have you marching with your hands tied behind your back. But Trommel snapped the case shut and came over with it to Major Widdicombe.

'Major, you left this in the grass.'

Trommel handed over the case with a little bow, very correctly. Major Widdicombe reached up and took it with some embarrassment.

'Thanks,' he said, and after a pause he opened the case and proffered it.

'Here,' he said disappointedly. 'You'd better have one, damn it.'

He lighted Major Trommel's cigarette and gazed morosely into the water, which was barely deep enough to cover his ankles.

'Your feet hurt you, Major?' Trommel inquired; Widdicombe sighed and nodded.

'Flat feet,' he said. 'When I first joined the army the M.O. told me he'd never seen anything remotely resembling my feet. Flatter than a camel's, that's what he said. My Aunt Ruth had flat feet, and it must have come out in me; that's what my mother used to say.'

Major Trommel said, 'I too am afflicted. I have a—a hen's breast.'

'Eh?'

Widdicombe looked carefully at Major Trommel's chest and said, 'Oh yes, I see. A pigeon-chest, we call it. Pity, that.'

They nodded and clicked their tongues commiseratingly

at each other, then lapsed into silence; Trommel stubbed out his cigarette.

'I must say I hadn't noticed your chest before, Major,' said Widdicombe. 'If it's any comfort to you, it looks almost normal to me.'

'Thank you,' said Trommel. 'Nor would I have guessed that there was anything the matter with your feet.'

'Well, thanks. . . . Here, have another cigarette, do. I've got plenty.'

They smoked companionably. Eventually Widdicombe said, 'Funny sort of set-up, wasn't it, leaving just the two of you at the village? You must have been well under strength.'

Trommel said, 'That is quite correct. There were twelve others: three non-commissioned officers and nine men.'

'Where did they get to?'

'I wish I knew,' Trommel said sadly. 'I suppose they will have been captured or killed. The front line has been swinging back and forth like the pendulum of a clock. I sent three men out to fetch rations six weeks ago. In two days they did not return, so I sent three more men, and so on. And in the end only myself and Wohlhaber were left to represent the occupying power.'

'Why didn't you just clear out?'

'That would have been unthinkable,' Major Trommel said indignantly. 'Desert my post? Borgo San Marco is a forgotten village, of no strategical or tactical importance, but I was ordered to occupy it, and that is what I did. You have shot my radio to pieces, and long before that I collected all the sets in the village and destroyed them—orders again, you understand—but Borgo San Marco is not only forgotten by the world, it has almost forgotten the world itself.'

Major Widdicombe grunted, then called to Sergeant

Entwistle and ordered him to see that the others were ready to move on in five minutes. Entwistle saluted and moved off. There was a hum of insects in the air, seeming louder now that Trommel had stopped talking. Widdicombe glanced covertly at him, wondering whether he could pump the man about the Countess and that oil she'd always been on about. Not that it mattered now: they'd never see her again, but just out of curiosity . . .? God, that noise—a droning buzz; must be some damned huge bluebottle. Still, the Countess. . . .

He tapped Major Trommel on the shoulder.

'I say, Major. Something I wanted to ask you . . .'

Trommel was staring up into the sky, his face pale and his mouth open in horror. Slowly, seeming half paralysed, he raised a hand and pointed.

Sergeant Entwistle shouted, 'Aircraft above, sir! Everybody scatter!'

The drone became a whine, then a screaming roar as the plane dived, flattened out, banked sharply: Major Widdicombe saw little puffs of smoke at the leading edges of the wings and a ferocious painted shark's head of teeth on the nose; and then he was lying in the rivulet with his arms over his head as the cannon-shells exploded along the road, crescendo and then diminuendo. Major Widdicombe raised his head, sneezing a blast of spray from his nostrils, and saw the plane come round in a tight turn.

'It's coming back,' he yelled. 'Keep down!'

He experienced a sudden overmastering anger and rolled on his back as the plane came in, this time in a flatter dive, firing a couple of staccato bursts from a hundred feet up. Widdicombe dragged out his revolver, thumbing off the safety catch and firing the rounds which remained in the gun, oblivious of the roar of the cannon-shells. He had emptied the chamber by the time he noticed the R.A.F.

roundels on the wings of the plane, all his earlier attention having been caught by the shark's head device.

The aircraft zoomed skywards, and Widdicombe lay with the back of his head in the water, remarking in the detachment induced by action how delightfully cool felt the bruise he had received the previous night.

'It's one of ours!' he said incredulously, watching the plane. 'The rotten filthy bastard.'

A thin dark streamer suddenly started from the underside of the engine cowling, the shark exhaling smoke. The plane climbed, circling to gain height; the streamer of smoke became a plume, the plume developed a red centre of flame; and in a few moments a shape like a blossoming white chrysanthemum was drifting down in the distance, falling gently out of sight behind the last foothills. The abandoned aircraft became a far-off comet dwindling in the eastern haze, the sound of its labouring engine lost among the rumbling of the guns; Widdicombe knew that it must have crashed, but heard nothing.

Major Trommel emerged from the stream behind Widdicombe and said suavely, 'One Kittyhawk of the Desert Air Force to your credit, Major. Allow me to tender my felicitations.'

Corporal White said to Sergeant Entwistle, 'First he loses a three-tonner all except for the chassis, and now he shoots a Kittyhawk down with a three-eight revolver. You know a Kittyhawk cosses somewhere round about a hundred and fifty thousand quid?'

'I know, Blacky,' Sergeant Entwistle said. 'You got to hand it to him, even if he is an officer. I mean it's the scale he works on; I swear to God I'm almost beginning to get to like him. Now get this: we didn't see nothing, no more did Dorbell, wherever he is.'

White nodded.

'Right,' he said. 'Back him up if it comes to the push, eh?'

They joined the officers. Wohlhaber was standing impassively behind Major Trommel, and Major Widdicombe was trying to reload his revolver from the little ammunition pouch on his service belt, spilling cartridges into the grass and moaning softly to himself.

Sergeant Entwistle said, 'Cheer up, sir. We never saw nothing, not a thing, but that was marvellous shooting, tamam bloody awi awi!'

Behind them the bedroll heaved, lurched aside, and Dorbell emerged. Corporal White said, 'Come over here, Knocker. You all right?'

Dorbell shambled over to them nodding palely.

'Did you see anything, Dorbell?' Sergeant Entwistle asked.

'Who, me, Sarge? No, I was under the major's kit.'

'Good,' said Entwistle. He winked at Major Widdicombe and said, 'Yer laughing, sir.'

Major Trommel said spitefully, 'On the contrary. I saw the major shoot down one of his own aircraft, and Private Wohlhaber will corroborate this. It will be worth while to be a prisoner of war in order to have the pleasure of giving evidence at his *Kriegsgericht*—how do you say?—martial court.'

'Court-martial,' Major Widdicombe said. 'But that's downright mean, after I gave you cigarettes and everything!'

Major Trommel smirked.

'This is war, Major,' he said. 'I must have some recompense for the loss of my liberty. Should you lose yours for a few years in one of your military detention centres, that will be tat for tit.'

Major Widdicombe gazed at Trommel in perplexity,

then bent and picked up the spilled cartridges. He straightened up showing a sudden resolution.

'Not on your life,' he said. 'Not on your Teutonic puff. I need some time to think this over, and you two are going right back to Borgo San Marco. . . . Prisoners and escort, about turn!'

*   *   *

When the party returned to the village the square was deserted and in twilight; the façade of the palazzo looming above lay in deep shadow; and from some house nearby leaked a pervasive smell of food: meat cooking with rosemary, probably dog. Major Widdicombe suddenly realised that he was ravenous. He halted everyone, wiped the sweat from his face, and walked limping to the command post, peering inside and returning at last with a complacent air.

'Sergeant,' he said, 'I'm turning that place into a guardroom for the prisoners.'

'But we have given our parole,' Major Trommel protested. 'And all our things are at the palazzo.'

'I'm moving you because I don't like your attitude, Major. A few days in there may help you to modify it, don't you think? Don't worry, I'll have your things sent over. Sergeant Entwistle will mount guard while the others prepare supper.' He turned to Corporal White and said, 'We'll have some of those tins of chicken suprême, Corporal. Oh, um yes, and mushroom soup to start off with, hey? Then after the chicken you can lash out some crêpes suzettes.'

'Mushroom soup, chicken suprême, crêpes suzettes. Very good, sir.'

Major Trommel stood in the odour of the cooking meat:

whatever it was, it had set him off salivating and swallowing.

Widdicombe said heartily, 'That's right, Corporal, don't stint yourself now. Dismiss, and take Dorbell with you. After he's made up my bed he can give you a hand. And see you invite the Countess to eat with us—after all, we'll be using her dining room.'

Major Trommel said, 'I can see you propose to starve us. That is a war crime. Er—not that I cannot endure, you understand: I am an officer of the Wehrmacht, and used to hardship. But Wohlhaber—I must protest on his behalf.'

'Good heavens,' Widdicombe said. 'You've got hold of the wrong end of the stick. Don't worry: I'll see you're fed.' Major Trommel brightened until Widdicombe went on, 'Whoever comes to relieve the sergeant will bring some corned beef and biscuits. And some water. Very nourishing, corned beef. So are the biscuits from all accounts. They say you can crack 'em if you jump up and down on them for an hour or two.'

Major Trommel stamped his foot and shouted, 'This is intolerable!'

'You should have thought a bit more before you began talking about giving evidence at my court-martial. Come on now.'

Sergeant Entwistle said, 'There's some guns in that strongpoint, sir. I'll disarm them heavy M.G.s if you could take the small arms away with you.'

*   *   *

Corporal White and Private Dorbell were already at work when Major Widdicombe entered the courtyard of the palazzo festooned with Schmeisser machine-pistols. They had set up the cooker close to the fountain, and

48

Widdicombe sniffed with delight as he passed the big canteen of mushroom soup. Gina was stirring it with Filomena looking on, but when the major appeared Filomena shot inside through the kitchen doorway, and Widdicombe heard her shrill voice squeaking excitedly before him. He dumped the weapons beside a brocaded chair in the hall, then sat down and took out his cigarette case, thinking. Back again, what a bloody day, still, put it over that stiff-necked Jerry all right.

He lighted a cigarette, looking up through wreathing smoke to see the Countess appear with Filomena, who slipped past with a giggle and a sideways glance at Major Widdicombe; the Countess sailed forward formally in a blue satin evening gown, holding out a hand in front of her, high up. Widdicombe kissed it.

'Welcome, welcome,' the Countess said, and then declaimed:

> ' "Ma misi per me l'alto mare aperto
> sol con un legno a con quella compagna
> picciola, dalla qual non fui deserto." '

Major Widdicombe said, 'Eh?'

'Dante. Like Ulysses, you have been away with your little faithful band. But now you have returned to your Penelope.'

Absolutely doolally, Major Widdicombe thought. Still, a good hot bath. . . . No, can't have that, just have to bathe my feet for now. . . . Food, a spot of Scotch, and then those transports of rapture.

'Well yes,' he said. 'Yes, I suppose you might put it like that. Had a tough time. I—er, shot down an aeroplane, by the way,' he added modestly.

The Countess beamed, taking his arm and leading him to the dining room.

'*Magnifico*,' she said. 'So brave, and so distinguished! Filomena told me you were coming with an armful of German guns.'

Widdicombe said, 'Oh, those. We didn't capture those, just took them out of Trommel's command post. I've stuck him in there under guard. Between you and me, he was getting much too far above himself.'

The Countess frowned and took her hand from his arm, then sat abstractedly at the table, fiddling with a silver salt cellar.

'Under guard?' she said. 'And . . . the private soldier?'

'Him too. Don't want him messing about making trouble. Though I must say he was very well behaved all day; hardly a word to say for himself. Why, you'd have thought he was leaving wife and home or something like that.'

'Mm. Yes,' said the Countess. 'It is not very civilised, I think, what you have done.'

Her manner was perceptibly colder. Widdicombe licked his lips and then said, 'Well, of course, I'm not leaving them there for ever, but that chap Trommel just got too big for his boots. Which reminds me: would it incommode you if I were to bathe my feet while we have our supper?'

Crazy, the Countess thought, and said, 'Be comfortable.'

Major Widdicombe vanished briefly, then came back smiling.

'Just the job,' he said. 'Soup'll be here any second.'

Corporal White brought in the soup, followed by Private Dorbell with a large bowl of cold water. Major Widdicombe placed the bowl down carefully in front of his chair, removed shoes and stockings, and lowered his feet gently into the bowl, sighing ecstatically. Then he picked up his soup spoon and glanced at the Countess to see if she was ready. She dipped her spoon in the soup, sipped, and said, 'Perfect!'

'*Slurp*,' said Major Widdicombe.

Both he and the Countess were inordinately hungry, and the meal passed with little more than grunts and disjointed small talk. When they had finished, Major Widdicombe remembered Trommel and Wohlhaber. He dried his feet and called for clean stockings, changed them, put on his shoes and asked the Countess to excuse him. She nodded graciously.

'By the way,' Widdicombe asked, 'got any gin or Scotch left?'

The Countess said, 'There is not much gin. You remember, I told you last night I had too much.'

He paused and then grinned lustfully.

'You did, come to think of it. We've got some Scotch though?'

'Whisky? Yes, there is almost a full bottle.'

'Good,' said Major Widdicombe. 'I'll just toddle off and see to those Jerries and then I'll be back. We can have a drink and you can tell me all about that oil.'

He patted her cheek and she squeezed his fingers encouragingly. Down Rover! he thought, and left.

In the courtyard Corporal White was feeding the servant girls with chicken in the hope of favours to be received; Dorbell was dozing at the table with his head on his arms. He raised his head yawning as Major Widdicombe entered.

'Wake up, Dorbell,' Widdicombe said. 'Fetch a tin of bully and some biscuits.'

'Yessir.'

In the courtyard the distant rumble of guns seemed louder. Major Widdicombe said to Corporal White, who had followed them out, 'Has this row been going on very long?'

'No, sir. Firing's hotting up a lot now, though.'

They listened to the increasing roar of the guns; in the deep well of the courtyard they could see no flashes and no reflections of them on cloud, for the reason that there was no cloud.

'Oh well,' Major Widdicombe said. 'Better make my tour of inspection. Dorbell will relieve Sergeant Entwistle until midnight, then you take over, Corporal. Four hours on and eight hours off, got it?'

'Right, sir,' White said disgustedly. Midnight, he thought. Just when I'd hoped to be between the sheets with that bint, ole Phenomena. He turned and went back into the kitchen.

In the street leading to the square the noise seemed deafening: it came from the plain, where an action was obviously developing. And from the parapet of the square the sight was awesome, a confusion of flashing guns and the bright pecked lines of tracer criss-crossing under high motionless flares.

Major Widdicombe swallowed and then said, 'Jolly fine show. Eighth Army on the move, what?'

Private Dorbell considered and said, 'If they are, then they're moving back'ards.'

Widdicombe stared at the flashes.

'God, you're right. We'd better watch for a minute and see what's happening.'

Outside the command post Sergeant Entwistle was sleeping, dreaming of live-baiting for pike. He had been singing happily for a while, listening with half an ear to enraged sounds from Major Trommel within, and with the other half to the increasing gunfire down in the plain, then had dozed off, weary after the long day's march. And inside the command post Major Trommel was busy making a Molotov cocktail with an empty bottle of schnaps.

'See, Wohlhaber,' he was saying, 'here is a bottle.'

Wohlhaber nodded, thinking, He's going to make a Molotov cocktail, I bet.

'What am I going to do with the bottle, Wohlhaber?'

'I've no idea, sir.'

'Fetch me the first-aid box.'

Major Trommel opened the box and took out a wad of cotton wool, laying it on the table.

'Now then, Wohlhaber, fetch the paraffin and petrol cans.'

The generator ran on a mixture of paraffin and petrol. Wohlhaber brought in two jerricans, and Major Trommel filled the bottle with petrol, wiping it meticulously afterwards. Then he recorked it and fastened the wad of cotton wool to its side with a strip of adhesive tape.

'Well,' he said. 'Now do you know what I am doing?'

'If the major permits. . . . It looks like a Molotov cocktail.'

'It *is* a Molotov cocktail,' Major Trommel said, soaking the wad with paraffin.

'Terrible things those are, sir,' Wohlhaber said. 'Seen them in Russia. You'll make a horrible mess of that Tommy.'

'Idiot!' said Major Trommel. 'You have no flexibility of mind. See. That is a door.' He pointed. 'Made of wood. Like your head. And outside the door is the English sergeant.'

'The major is going to set fire to the door?' Wohlhaber inquired.

Trommel groaned with exasperation.

'No. I am going to make that sergeant open the door, and then I am going to light this thing and throw it at the barber's shop. The shop will burn, the sergeant will call for help, and in the confusion we will run for it. I no longer consider myself, or you, bound by parole, and it is therefore our bounden duty to escape. Are you ready?'

Wohlhaber nodded.

Trommel took out a box of matches and said, 'When I say the word, scream as loud as you can. Imagine the Cossacks are chasing you or something like that.'

He struck a match and held it ready.

*   *   *

The guns boomed and the tracer flicked across the plain under the flares, and by their light Major Widdicombe saw the squat black shape come round the bend and climb towards Borgo San Marco, rattling and roaring, the enormous length of the 88 mm. gun protruding before it.

Dorbell said, 'That's a tank, sir. Is it one of ours?'

Major Widdicombe stared, recalling pictures of precisely such tanks.

He said in horror, 'It's a Tiger tank!'

'Yes, sir, but is it one of ours?' Dorbell said patiently.

The tank was approaching inexorably below them. Major Widdicombe tore himself from the parapet.

'The command post,' he yelled. 'Try and get a machine-gun armed again.'

As he ran across the square he heard a yell, saw Entwistle start to his feet and fling open the door of the command post. He was some yards away when a flaming meteor hissed through the air above his head and vanished over the parapet. Major Widdicombe hauled out his revolver and charged into the command post, where Major Trommel and Private Wohlhaber were standing with an air of expectancy which changed to consternation as Widdicombe entered.

Widdicombe shouted, 'Sergeant, stand those two over there in the corner. The enemy are down below. Can we get one of these guns working?'

'Not a hope, sir,' Entwistle said. 'They're proper zifti. Fixed 'em meself.'

'Oh, damn it!'

Major Widdicombe rushed to a machine-gun embrasure and peered through the slit, his eyes widening. Then he straightened up and turned to Major Trommel.

'Did you throw that thing?'

Trommel smirked, putting a good face on failure. He shrugged.

'A little ruse, one might say. It did not come off, which was a pity. But there was no harm done. My Molotov cocktail might have hit you, Major, and I must ask you to believe that this was not my intention. I was aiming at the barber's shop.'

Major Widdicombe beckoned silently, and Trommel came forward. Still unspeaking, Widdicombe gestured at the embrasure, and Trommel bent to look through it. Together they gazed down on the flaming tank, seeing the tiny figures running down the road from it in the light of the conflagration. The tracks were blazing, and the fire had spread all round; from inside the tank various muffled pops and bangs could be heard. Major Trommel's brow was suddenly sequined by the sweat of fear. Entwistle, Dorbell and Wohlhaber joined the officers, peering out and murmuring with astonishment.

'*My* turn to congratulate *you*,' Major Widdicombe said. 'You and Mr Molotov, of course. I think you two might be safer up at the palazzo.'

Major Trommel gave a shuddering sigh and mopped his forehead.

'I shall be only too happy to renew our parole.'

'I'll bet you will,' said Widdicombe. 'Come along then.'

Private Dorbell watched the officers and Wohlhaber move off, then turned to Sergeant Entwistle and said hopefully, 'Does that mean I'm excused guard duty, Sarge?'

'No, it does not. You stop here and watch the road. And don't you take your eyes off it, understand?'

Sergeant Entwistle hurried off to catch up the others as they walked through the square in a buzz of excited conversation from the villagers who had gathered there. Major Trommel was muttering to himself in German and Major Widdicombe was humming, anticipating transports of rapture. Neither of them noticed Filomena hurrying ahead of them; but when Major Widdicombe reached the palazzo, the Countess was nowhere to be found. And very soon, neither was Private Wohlhaber.

5

PRIVATE DORBELL stared dutifully at the road below the command post until midnight, when Corporal White relieved him. The corporal was in a sour mood because Filomena was still holding out against all his blandishments. The night before, he had managed to entice her to his room under the pretext that he would show her some jewellery; but the air-strike in the plain had interrupted matters. And now came this blasted guard duty, just at the wrong moment. Dorbell left; Corporal White glowered grumpily into the darkness lighted by the gun-flashes, which had receded now: the tank below could be discerned only fitfully. But the wind had changed, and blew a stench of smouldering rubber into the command post, making the corporal cough and spit through the embrasure.

In the palazzo Major Widdicombe lay in bed awaiting the Countess. She was certainly taking her time. He smoked several cigarettes, fighting against the sleep which threatened to overwhelm him. Perhaps the Countess had been annoyed because he had forgotten to give her drinks before retiring. A little nightcap. He rose from the bed, switched on his torch, and put on his khaki drill slacks; the night had become cool and his shorts were begrimed by the previous day's happenings. Then he put on a shirt and went down stealthily to the dining room, finding the whisky bottle and taking two glasses back upstairs with it. But where did the Countess sleep? He paused uncertainly at the head of the wide stairway, his torch hand resting on the marble rail of the balustrade, the bottle and glasses clutched in the other, and saw Major Trommel moving down the corridor on tiptoe, his back to Widdicombe. Trommel was wearing a nightshirt patterned with green and orange lozenges, and he carried a candle. He paused at one of the bedroom doors, tapped softly, opened the door, and vanished from sight.

Major Widdicombe sidled along the landing and peeped into the room, the beam of his torch passing across a ceiling painted with a fat Virgin and Child among an assortment of fat *putti*. Major Trommel was holding the candle high in the air and staring at the huge, empty bed, clicking his tongue dolefully, when the torch beam lanced over his shoulder and made a yellow blob of light on the wall behind the bed. Trommel spun round, hissing as he spilt candlegrease on his wrist, blinking as his eyes were held in the dazzle.

'And what the hell are you up to?' Major Widdicombe asked. 'Sneaking about in the middle of the night.'

Major Trommel moved out of the beam of light and said with some attempt at dignity, 'Does that concern you? As you see, I am not dressed for escaping. I am—er, that is to say I was—er, I could not sleep. Wohlhaber always brings me my little glass of warm water at midnight, but tonight he did not bring it.'

'Doesn't sleep here, does he? This is a very splendid sort of room—not the sort of place for one's servant, surely?'

Major Trommel shook his head in confusion, and Widdicombe suddenly felt sorry for him. Poor bloody old idiot standing there like a plucked turkey in a jester's outfit.

'Here,' he said, 'for heaven's sake park that candle and sit down. I haven't any warm water, but this stuff's just the job for insomnia. My trouble's going to be staying awake.'

He poured whisky into the glasses while Major Trommel made a little pool of molten grease in an ashtray and stood the candle in it, then accepted his whisky gratefully, sipped, gasped, and sat down on a chintzy ottoman. Widdicombe sat on an upholstered stool which he pulled from its place near the dressing table.

'We're in a fix,' he said at length. 'Ever thought about that?'

He fumbled in the pocket of his shirt, brought out a packet of cigarettes and tossed one to Major Trommel, lighting his own in the candle flame; Trommel did the same, his cheeks hollow pits as he inhaled.

'A fix,' Trommel said, sitting down again. 'I have been thinking about nothing else.'

'Well, I'm a sight worse off than you are. That pilot got away. What if he saw that I was British? And what if my men rat on me? Mind you, I'm pretty sure of them. I don't think they'd ever give me away intentionally, but you know how it is: they start drinking beer in the N.A.A.F.I., and before you know where you are the cat's out of the bag. Big joke—officer shot down a Kittyhawk with a pistol, and so on. I swear to God I didn't know it was a British plane, and I just loosed off blindly. Damn it, the whole thing was an accident. . . . But who the hell will ever believe that?' he said gloomily. 'And if it'd take five years to pay for that three-tonner, I'd have to sign up till bloody doomsday to pay for a Kittyhawk.'

Major Trommel nodded sympathetically.

'An accident,' he said. 'It was the same with me. But Wohlhaber saw the whole thing—quite apart from you people. Wohlhaber means well, but he forgets things.'

'He might forget about that tank.'

'No,' Major Trommel said, shaking his head. 'That is the kind of thing he can be counted upon to remember. That's the trouble with Wohlhaber.'

'Here, have a spot more whisky,' Widdicombe said, topping up the glasses. He swished his whisky round in the glass. 'You know, all this is a hell of a disappointment. I've not been in Italy for a week yet, and there I was with two prisoners. Why, if I'd managed to get you two to Eighth Army Headquarters there'd have been no cracks about getting my knees brown; they could have been as white as a virgin's wedding dress, and who'd have cared?'

Major Trommel looked puzzled by Widdicombe's last words, but nodded just the same

'These wretched flat feet,' said Widdicombe, kicking one against the other. 'If it hadn't been for my feet I'd have been out here years ago, or somewhere—and in the infantry too.'

'I know how you feel,' Major Trommel told him. 'Just the same with my chest. Always stuck me somewhere out of the way. I am a good Aryan type, is that not so?' he demanded aggrievedly.

Widdicombe looked at Major Trommel and decided that he resembled a bald and bleached American Indian eighty years old, and said, 'I suppose so. Not that I know much about it. Seems a proper old load of balls when you come to think of it. Take your chap Hitler for instance. How Aryan does *he* look?'

'*Himmelheiligergottkreuzsakramentendonnerwetterfeuer!*' Major Trommel said, excited. 'I had never thought of that.'

'You do. You have a good big think about it. And another thing,' Widdicombe said. 'You don't pull a trigger with your chest, any more than I use my feet. Damn it all, I've shot down a plane and you've knocked out a tank. What if the plane had been German and the tank British? We'd each be a bloody hero. Have some more whisky.'

Major Trommel drained his glass and held it out for more. He said, 'That is English sophistry. The plane was not an enemy plane and the tank was not an enemy tank: therefore we should not be heroes in the eyes of our commanders, but criminals.'

'Try seeing our point of view,' Widdicombe suggested. 'From the military angle, the plane and the tank just about cancel each other out. The balance or preponderance of material is just what it was before. But on the personal level, by God, I've *done* something, and so have you. Why get all down in the dumps? Speaking for myself, I feel a sight more cheerful now.'

Extraordinary business, he thought. Doing some proper thinking: never dreamed I had it in me. He watched Major Trommel frown in the flickering candlelight, then brighten and cackle quietly.

'Major, you are right!' Trommel said. 'Personal achievement is what counts. I have not fired a shot in anger since 1941, and that was at Libyan near Bir el Gubi. He stole my blankets. And I missed him.' He sat upright on the ottoman, clutching his glass in one hand and slapping his knee with the other. 'It was a fine sight, *prachtvoll*, all those flames jumping out of that tank!'

'I know,' said Widdicombe. 'Jolly fine show. And I'll never forget that plane roaring away on fire there like a bloody comet or something!'

'Memorable,' Major Trommel said. 'Memorable is the word that hits the head right upon the nail. Sticking me away in these outposts where nothing ever happens! That will show them.'

'Yes, and what action would I have seen in charge of a mess hall at Main Eighth Army?' Widdicombe demanded. 'Have another drink.'

'*Prosit.*'

'*Prosit.*'

'Cheers.'

'Cheers.'

'Look,' said Widdicombe eagerly. 'I know what. Let's pretend that you shot down that plane and I knocked out the tank. Right?'

'Very well,' Trommel said. 'It is a game? I shot down the plane.'

'What sort of medal do you think you ought to have?'

Trommel drank, considered.

'Oh, a *Ritterkreuz*. With swords and oak leaves.'

'Right. And I should think they'd lash out a Military Cross for that tank. Major Trommel, consider yourself entitled to—er, whatever it was you said.'

'And you, Major, to the Military Cross. Very gallantly earned, if I may say so,' Trommel said, patting Major Widdicombe's shoulder.

'Well, thanks. Jolly decent of you. Have another drink.'

They sipped owlishly; Major Widdicombe gave Major Trommel another cigarette, and the smoke from his own rose in the still air and mingled with Major Trommel's in a tenuous symbol of unity.

'What did you do before the war?' Major Trommel asked.

'Eh? Oh, I kept a pub.'

'A pub,' said Trommel. 'I have heard of those, but I have never seen one.'

'Nice little place near Exmouth. Lots of holiday trade, but we've got a good steady local trade too: regulars—

you know—darts and shove ha'penny teams. Not much catering except in summer and my mother and my Aun Ruth used to see to that. Auntie died last winter, though, and Mother's trying to hold the fort by herself. . . . Wha did you do?'

'I was a *Beamter*,' Trommel said. 'A civil servant. It was good enough until the big inflation came, and then those of us on fixed salaries were ruined.' He shrugged. 'It was a dull life, I suppose, till the war came.'

Major Widdicombe stared into his glass, and then said to himself aloud, 'Save a lot of trouble.'

'I beg your pardon?'

'Oh, just thinking,' he said with pride. 'Strornry how these ideas come. Stead of having a war, see? Each side collects all its tanks and planes and so forth, then each side bashes hell out of its own stuff. Save no end of bother.' He puzzled for a moment and then shook his head. 'No, it wouldn't work. I've gone off the track somewhere. Trouble is we're fighting against all that cock about Aryans and master-races. You know what I think? I think that little bugger Hitler with his black hair and those eyes and that shape of head—I think he's a diddicoy.'

'Diddicoy?'

'Kind of a half-breed gipsy.'

Major Trommel puckered his lips and blew gently through them, standing and goggling at Widdicombe.

'A gipsy? The Führer?'

'No, a diddicoy. Oh well, I s'pose gipsy's near enough for you, but it's not what I mean. What I mean is that he could be half-Austrian or Hungarian or Russian as well as gipsy . . .'

'A gipsy!' Major Trommel said aghast. 'Half-Hungarian, half-Russian!'

'Sticks out a mile,' Major Widdicombe said with complacency. 'God, man: think what he looks like. Where's your blond beast? Tell me that.'

Major Trommel shook his head helplessly.

Widdicombe said, 'And I think he's a bloody fool into the bargain.'

Trommel sat down suddenly and said, 'Pfuiii!' Then he giggled and said in a whisper, looking round furtively, 'The Führer is a bloody fool.' He held on to his seat with both hands and with his teeth clenched, but nothing happened: no Gestapo materialising from the shadows, no horde of Valkyries storming through the ceiling. Major Trommel shouted, 'The Führer is a bloody fool!' Then he turned back to Widdicombe and said, 'That will teach him leaving me to rot in a place like this with my capacity for soldierly conduct, shooting down enemy aeroplanes.' He shook Major Widdicombe's hand and said, 'Major, you have taught me a great deal. It is an ill wind that has no turning.'

Major Widdicombe said, 'Funny thing, that. If you can do it, so can the others. By God, if we tell 'em often enough and long enough they'll end up believing that you shot down the plane and I knocked out the tank. Have to stay here for a bit, though: play for time. If I can remember about this in the morning we might give it a try.'

He ushered Major Trommel to the door and bade him goodnight, standing in the doorway and lighting Trommel along the corridor by torchlight until the green and orange patterned back had vanished from sight. Widdicombe turned back into the room, fetched the whisky bottle and the glasses, and went downstairs to return them to the dining room, walking slowly and deliberately. There was perhaps an eggcupful of whisky left in the bottle. Back outside his own room again, he yawned and ran a hand through his hair, blinking with drowsiness. He opened the door, and as he passed over the threshold he heard a sound from down the corridor. Peeping round the door-jamb he saw the figure of the Countess at the stairhead. She moved along the corridor humming softly and contentedly to herself, visible only as a black bulk of denser quality than the rest of the gloom. She opened a door and disappeared just as Major Widdicombe was about to give a loud hiss by way of announcing his presence.

Funny, Widdicombe thought. She's gone into that room with all those fat babies and things painted on the ceiling Follow her?

He pondered briefly, then decided against it: too much whisky inside himself, not enough for the Countess. Tomorrow was another day. Widdicombe splashed his face with cold water, brushed his teeth, then undressed quickly and lay in bed, eyes closed and sleep roaring in on him like a tiger; his last coherent thought was no more than a snippet of puzzlement why Major Trommel should have been in that room.

6

PRIVATE DORBELL sat morosely at the kitchen table at seven-thirty on the following morning, Corporal White opposite him chewing toast loudly. Dorbell gazed at the artificial flowers in their fat terra cotta vase, ignoring Gina and Filomena as they bustled about setting out breakfast for the Countess and the officers.

'What's up with you then, Knocker?'

Dorbell removed his gaze from the flowers.

'Goin's-on,' he said. 'That's what's up. You ought to know, and that there lass ought to be ashamed. Coming rooning through me bedroom at four-thirty in the morning with you after her.'

He looked sourly at the trim figure of Filomena as she spooned scrambled egg on to slices of toast, while Corporal White smacked his lips and said, 'And I'll catch her yet, never you fear. *Then* she'll have something to be ashamed of.'

Dorbell sighed and then said hopefully, 'Can I lend you a boook, Corp?'

'What is it?'

'It'd do you good. It's a boook called *The Wages of Sin.*'

'I'm on time and a half already,' Corporal White said, and buttered another slice of toast. 'Pass that tin of marmalade.'

Dorbell slid the tin along the table. He said, 'I do wish this war 'ud hurry up and finish so I can get back in the Army. Eee, I do miss me Sundy mornings and me chooba.'

'You mean you used to play one of them things?'

Private Dorbell nodded and said, 'Aye, I did and all. Our band was a treat. When we played "Onward, Christian Soldiers" at the corner of Station Road in Ardwick they could hear us by the gasworks in Oom.'

'Oom?'

'Aitch-you-ell-em-ee,' Dorbell said patiently. 'Oom.'

He took his plates over to the sink and plonked them down hastily near Filomena. She smiled nicely at him and he blushed crimson to the tips of his ears, scuttling back to the table.

'Got to get ready,' he said to Corporal White. 'Got to relieve Sarge at eight.'

'Don't put your face too close to that tank, then,' White said, 'or the bleeding thing'll go up in flames all over again.'

*　　　　*　　　　*

The tank had stopped burning when Dorbell reached the parapet at the far end of the village square. Two old men in black cloaks sat on rush-bottomed chairs outside the inn, gossiping, presumably having been ejected early by their womenfolk. A thickset middle-aged man was holding the nozzle of the petrol pump over the tank of a decrepit motor-cycle, shouting curses while alternately kicking the base of the pump and shaking the nozzle. A dozen dogs yelped across the square in pursuit of a small and dirty but evidently desirable bitch; Dorbell permitted himself a comparison between the dogs and his own comrades-in-arms, peered lackadaisically over the parapet and saw a group of small boys clambering over the tank and snapping forefinger guns at one another. An individualist of five or six years came past him shuffling his feet and chuffing, blowing an imaginary whistle and intoning, '*Parto per Napoli!*'

The man at the petrol pump dropped the dry nozzle in the dust and wheeled his contraption over to Dorbell, smiling and saying, 'Good day, sir. Have you perhaps a little petrol for the machine?'

'Wasky most,' said Dorbell firmly.

'The Germans have petrol for their generator,' the man told him, each word in Italian carefully enunciated. 'As a co-belligerent, surely I might be permitted to borrow half a litre?'

Dorbell said, 'I don't know what you're on about with your mithering in Eyetie. Why don't you see the sergeant?'

The man said, 'Perhaps I might see the sergeant?' and walked along with Dorbell to the command post, leaning his motor-cycle against the wall. 'Soon,' he said, 'the war will be over, and everybody will be equal. Doubtless I myself shall drive an Alfa-Romeo. *A basso i grandi capi!*'

Dorbell said, 'The sergeant's in here. He speaks a bit of Eyetie, and that's a blessing.'

Sergeant Entwistle glanced up from an old copy of *The Crusader* as Dorbell came in with the man.

'Who's this, then?'

The Italian said, 'For courtesy, I should like to borrow a small quantity of petrol: a half-litre—a litre, perhaps? I wish to visit my old mother, down there.'

He pointed through the machine-gun embrasure to the plain.

'Well, I'm allah-keefik,' Sergeant Entwistle said. 'Scout round at the back, Knocker, and see if you can find him a drop of juice. He wants to go and see his old ma.'

Dorbell filled the man's petrol tank from a jerrican, waved aside his thanks, and then went back inside the command post. Outside, the motor-cycle coughed and spat a few times, then set up a steady popping roar.

'Aunt Maria's jackdaw,' Sergeant Entwistle said as the engine noise diminished gradually into the distance. 'All twitter and you-know-what, not that I'd offend your little swill bucket of a mind, Dorbell. Now you get sat in that chair till twelve hundred hours, and if nothing's happened by then, I'm going to ask the major to drop this sentry duty and let us all get back to normal, whatever that is.'

*   *   *

Major Widdicombe slept late, waking just after ten o'clock with a headache and a sour taste in the mouth. He was dressing and yawning, scratching his stomach and trying to piece together his fragmented memories of the night, thinking that Major Trommel wasn't such a bad stick after all, when a tap came at the door and Wohlhaber entered, carrying a tray on which stood a mug of coffee and a jug of hot water for shaving. He clicked his heels, proffering the tray silently.

'Well I say,' Widdicombe said. 'That *is* decent. From Major Trommel, I take it?'

Wohlhaber nodded and said, '*Bitte schön.*'

Major Widdicombe thought, My God, he looks tired. Absolutely fagged out: look at those great dark bags under his eyes, never get those through the Customs, ha-ha. Expect old Trommel kept him up half the night waiting for him; he said something about the man last night but I'm buggered if I can remember what it was.

He gave Wohlhaber a cigarette. Wohlhaber tucked it away in the breast pocket of his uniform jacket, thanked

Widdicombe in German, and left the room, leaving Major Widdicombe to finish his toilet and drink his coffee. Then Widdicombe trotted downstairs, feeling restored and shouting into the kitchen for his breakfast: toast and marmalade, bacon and egg—tinned bacon and dehydrated egg. He took the food into the morning room and was surprised to find the Countess sitting there with Major Trommel. Trommel rose and bowed as Widdicombe came in; the Countess held out a languid hand for him to kiss. He thought, She looks absolutely in the pink, positively blossoming: look at those marvellous eyes. That's where she got to last night; ten hours' beauty sleep at least, I bet. Old Trommel and I must have wakened her up, though, and she must have gone to that room to check up.

He said, 'Good morning, Countess. 'Morning, Major—thanks for having your man bring me a cup of coffee, set me up no end.'

'It was a pleasure,' Trommel said.

'Hope you don't mind if I have my breakfast in here?'

Major Trommel shook his head, and the Countess said throatily, 'Please do, Major. A woman likes to watch her guests eat, if they are men.'

Widdicombe grinned delightedly, retrieved his breakfast and began to eat while the Countess watched him with solicitude.

'Ah!' she said, her eyes fixed on Major Widdicombe's stolidly moving jaws. 'That is how a man should eat: with love, with application. I declare, Major Widdicombe, you eat almost as well as my Federico used to. . . . There is a saying current among the peasants that the English do not possess teeth, that they are born toothless. I do not think they could say that of you.'

Major Widdicombe swallowed, beamed and said, 'No indeed. Got thirty-two. Not as pretty as yours, though.'

'Compliments all round,' Major Trommel said with a touch of acidity, and the Countess turned to him lazily.

'Now as for yourself, Major,' she said. 'I have noticed that you have a very small.'

'A very small?' Trommel said. 'That is not correct English. A very small what?'

'A very small appetite. Little, so'—the Countess enclosed a tiny space between thumb and forefinger—'as little as a pin's prick.'

Major Trommel said huffily, 'I do not agree. But I am bound to point out that there is no virtue of itself in eating great quantities of food.'

'Yes, yes!' the Countess crowed. 'But there is much. To eat well gives strength to a man, that is the point. Major Widdicombe has a big and strong, and you have only a little tiny small.'

Major Trommel said, 'You are against me after all, Sismonda. A weathercoat and a turncock.'

Nastily, the Countess said, 'Against you? How could you ever think I was for you? Such arrogance is typical. I may have admitted you under my roof, to my—my table, but you take too much upon yourself if you think that ever I did you more than the bare courtesy of hospitality to one I presumed was an officer and a gentleman.' Her voice rose: 'Am I to think perhaps I was mistaken in that?'

Bare courtesy, Trommel thought bitterly. That is a good one; famous. I could show her up now, but I won't, not after what she said about officers and gentlemen; that would be playing into her hands. Trommel spread out his fingers and said in a conciliatory tone, 'Let us not quarrel. As you were at pains to say, Major Widdicombe is enjoying his breakfast: let him continue to do so.'

'Jolly good idea,' Widdicombe said through an electric

crackle of toast. 'Just finish this, then we'll sit for a bit and have a smoke, eh, Major?'

Major Trommel smiled, mollified by this manifestation of comradeship in arms, and the Countess frowned. For a moment she seemed on the brink of some devastating statement to Major Trommel, but at length she subsided, sitting heavily back in her chair while Major Widdicombe finished his breakfast and drank his tea, sipping with noisy enjoyment. He set down the empty mug and offered cigarettes; the Countess shook her head.

'But do smoke, gentlemen,' she said sweetly. 'While Major Widdicombe digests his food I have something I wish to say to him.'

She leaned forward. Widdicombe gazed at her, mesmerised by her cleavage, which was enhanced by the low V-neck of her blue and white striped cotton frock.

The Great Divide, Widdicombe musēd, and said vaguely 'Yes, dear Countess, I'm all ears. Oh lord, the Grand Canyon.'

'Eh?' said the Countess and Major Trommel together.

'Sorry. Thinking of something else.'

Widdicombe lighted Major Trommel's cigarette and then his own, saying to the Countess, 'Sorry. Do go on.'

'Well,' she said, 'it is a matter of great concern to me, a matter of life and death for me and my poor village.'

'Yes,' Widdicombe said, still bemused. 'Borgo San Marco and all that.'

The Countess said, 'It is the oil.'

There she goes again, thought Widdicombe. On again about that oil; I'd forgotten all about it.

There she goes again, thought Trommel. The ever-womanly oil drags us upward. I thought she'd forgotten all about it.

There was a tap at the door, and Corporal White came in.

'Sorry to disturb you, sir,' he said to Widdicombe. 'Dorbell's brought some Italian bloke up here in a terrible state, and we can't make out what he's saying.'

Major Widdicombe said, 'I know. It's that Lancashire accent or whatever he's got. Tell him to speak a bit more quickly.'

'Not Dorbell, sir,' White said. 'This Italian. He came up here very quick on a motor-bike, with Dorbell on the back. This bloke's all excited, gabbling away, and the girls can't speak English so we can't tell what he's on about. Will you be coming down, sir?'

'Oh, all right,' Widdicombe said, and White saluted, spun on his heel, stamped boots, and went.

Major Trommel said, 'I will come with you, that is if you do not object. It may be important. You will forgive us, Sismonda?'

The Countess was seething. She shouted, 'Not once, not ever, does anybody listen to me about my oil. What can this man want which is capable of more importance than my oil?'

Widdicombe said soothingly, 'I'm sure you're quite right, dear lady. Now look: I'll have to see this fellow and find out what's the matter. Why don't you come along and help? Then, when this storm in a teacup has blown over, you can start straight away and tell me about the oil, hmm? That's a promise.'

He stood with an air of decision, and held open the door. The Countess breathed heavily, then got up, snorted, and led the way to the kitchen.

The place was crowded with people all talking at once. The thickset Italian was standing with Dorbell and Sergeant Entwistle, who was trying to slow down the man's speech; behind them stood White and Wohlhaber, while Gina and Filomena were flapping their arms at a couple of dozen villagers and trying to shoo them outside. The Countess sized up the situation, took a deep breath, then gave an ear-splitting shout; the noise of the others died away.

'Thanks very much,' Widdicombe said with respect. 'A Guards R.S.M. couldn't have done better than that.' He turned to Dorbell and asked, 'Now then, what's going on here?'

Dorbell pointed to the Italian motor-cyclist and said, 'It's this feller, sir. He went off on his motor-bike, and then he come back yelling and bellering. He keeps going on about some chap called Ted Esky. Ted Esky this and Ted Esky that: I wish he'd go away.'

Entwistle said, 'If he'd talk slower I might be able to get something out of him, but it's no use.'

'*Tedeschi?*' the Countess said sharply, and turned to the man, speaking rapidly. He nodded, gestured largely, and kept up a crossfire of voluble speech in answer to the Countess's questions. Eventually she cut him off with an imperious gesture and turned back to Major Widdicombe.

'It is bad news for you, Major,' she said, 'and good news for Major Trommel. It appears that the German counter-attack has been successful, and that German troops are in command of all the communications in the plain. He says that the Germans have dug in all the way across the road four miles from here, facing the coast.'

'Good heavens,' Widdicombe said. 'And we're behind them!'

The Countess nodded, the villagers buzzed. Major Trommel took a sudden step closer to Widdicombe and held out his hand.

'Your revolver, Major, if you please,' he said.

'Eh?'

Major Trommel smiled and said, 'It is simple. You

and your men are now my prisoners. Now—your revolver.'

'Oh, I say,' Widdicombe protested. His under-lip protruded, quivering. 'This is terrible.' He gazed at Trommel's outstretched hand, and then slowly drew his revolver, passing it over.

Major Trommel said gleefully, 'Aha. Now I am in command.' He yelled at the villagers, '*Hauen Sie mal ab! Via!*'

Some of the people filtered away, grumbling, but the rest stood their ground, including a fat woman in a black dress, who went to the kitchen table and picked up the terra cotta vase with the artificial flowers. Major Trommel turned and looked curiously at Wohlhaber, who was uttering small strangled noises. He patted Wohlhaber's shoulder and said, 'A great moment, is it not? Good, loyal fellow. But do not let it affect you too deeply.'

The fat woman gave the flowers to a little girl who stood behind her; the girl came forward and dropped a curtsey, handing the vase to Major Trommel. As he took it, the villagers left in the room raised a lugubrious cheer. Major Widdicombe had begun to cry quietly.

Wohlhaber's teeth were chattering. He shot to Major Trommel's side.

'Ah, you had better hold these,' Trommel said pleasantly.

Wohlhaber grabbed the vase, and Major Trommel glanced at him with renewed concern.

'My poor man,' he said sympathetically. 'All this has been too much for you, I can see. Now go and lie down until you feel better.'

Wohlhaber said, 'At once, sir,' and whipped out of the room, clutching the vase. The Countess looked after him with raised eyebrows, then spat some words of command to the remaining villagers, who moved through the outside door with a speed rivalling Wohlhaber's.

The Countess said equably, 'Ah, the joys and sorrows of life! Major Widdicombe was happy and Major Trommel was sad; but now Major Trommel is happy and Major Widdicombe is sad. *Porca miseria!* Fortune is fickle.'

Major Widdicombe sniffed.

Sergeant Entwistle said to Corporal White, 'Do something to get that Jerry's attention while I find me cleaver: I think it's in one of them drawers. I'll have his head off in one swipe bar-din.'

'Not me,' said Corporal White. 'I'm not getting shot, not for you I'm not, not while I get the bullet and you get the medal I'm bleeding not, no bleeding fear.'

'Coward.'

Corporal White said, 'That's right. I'd rather have a tuppenny stamp than a postoomious Victoria Cross any day.'

Major Trommel said to Widdicombe, who was standing drooped in complete dejection, 'I believe your sergeant is planning to attack me, Major. Kindly offer parole on behalf of yourself and your men, or I shall be compelled to place you all in close confinement.'

'Uh?' said Major Widdicombe hollowly, desolated. 'Eh? What? Oh yes, parole. Yes, I'll give parole for myself and these men. . . . Now just you stop it, Sergeant.'

He blew his nose; Sergeant Entwistle subsided, grumbling. Dorbell came forward timidly and tugged at Major Widdicombe's sleeve.

'Will we have to go to Germany, sir?' he asked. 'I've heard tell they eat nowt but sausages and drink beer all the time. I don't want to go to Germany and have nowt but sausages and beer.'

Sergeant Entwistle said, 'They'll put us up against a wall and shoot us, more like.'

Major Widdicombe looked at his men: Entwistle tough and defiant, White sharp-eyed for the main chance, Dorbell like a small hurt spaniel; and he felt a sudden upsurge of protective feeling for them which drowned his own self-pity.

He said, 'No, they won't. I'm your officer, and I'll see that nothing happens to you.'

Major Trommel said suavely, 'It is out of your hands, Major. You are my prisoner, remember?'

Widdicombe slapped his thigh and began to laugh. He said, 'So you don't want to play games any more? You'll take us in and hand us over? Three witnesses at *your* court-martial!'

Trommel blenched.

'I saw you knock out that Tiger tank; Dorbell saw you; so did Sergeant Entwistle. Take us in—and see what happens to you!'

'*Ach, Gott!*' said Major Trommel, striking himself on the side of the head with an open hand. He paused, and finally sighed. 'We remain here for the present. It is the only thing to do.'

'What if your people come here?' Widdicombe asked.

The Countess had been standing by in silent amusement, but now she said, 'If you stay here and the Germans come, you will both be in trouble. I have a plan. Let us go back upstairs, all three of us, and then I will tell you about the oil.'

7

THEY walked up to the drawing room, the Countess suddenly formal and distant, regally composed as she motioned Trommel and Widdicombe to a pair of straight-backed chairs. She herself remained standing.

Major Trommel said, 'Is my presence necessary? You know that I have heard before what you are going to say, and that I have not been impressed by your idea.'

'You have said yourself that the situation has changed,' the Countess reminded him. 'Now kindly keep silent while I explain my problem to Major Widdicombe.'

Guns had begun to rattle and thump once more down in the plain, but they took no notice. Major Widdicombe was fixed accurately this time by the lustrous wells of the Countess's eyes. He said, 'Please tell me.'

The Countess said, 'Borgo San Marco is a poor village, Major. Before the war we had a hard enough time, but since the war things have become impossible. No one ever comes here. Why should they? The road stops here. Everybody has forgotten about us. The war has destroyed our vines in the foothills, and we have no wine; our stocks of pasta are running out; petrol, soap, tobacco—these are memories to most of my poor villagers. And oil.'

Major Trommel groaned and shifted his position impatiently.

'I do not wish to listen to all this for the fiftieth time,' he said.

'Illiterate!' the Countess yelled at him. 'Keep quiet, or I will go myself down to the Germans, and then I will tell them all about you.'

Trommel said anxiously, 'Please continue, Countess.'

'There!' she said to Major Widdicombe. 'These Germans are all the same. One has to shout at them to secure acquiescence. . . . Now then: my poor dear Federico owned very large estates in the south, near Bitonto, with many fine olive groves. Up here the olive does not grow, so every spring our estate manager in the south sends a mule train with enough oil to last the village for the rest of the year. When Federico met his glorious end, I inherited the estates, and continued the custom.

'Oil is as necessary to us as the air we breathe, Major. My villagers use it for cooking, to drink in winter, to fill their lamps—for a hundred things.'

'Golly,' Major Widdicombe said. 'I didn't know that. Jolly interesting.'

Major Trommel risked a small sniff of contempt. Widdicombe took out his cigarette case and lighted a cigarette, pointedly leaving out Trommel.

The Countess smirked happily, then went on: 'The oil fruits are left on the tree until midwinter. By that time they have turned quite black, and their oil content is at its highest. Then the olives are picked and go to the mill, where they are crushed, and the oil is extracted, clarified and cleaned. It is then bottled or barrelled.' She paused, her face clouded, and she said, 'Every year in March the mules came in with thirty barrels of oil, every year since I married Federico.' Her voice rose to a rhetorical pitch: 'Every year since nineteen hundred and thirty-four the oil has come through. It has come through in the worst years of the war: nineteen forty-three, nineteen forty-four. But this year what has happened? March has been, April will soon be over, but the mules have not come. What will befall my *poverini* when they have no oil?'

She began to sob, and Major Widdicombe hastily stood, pulling out a clean handkerchief and giving it to her.

'Here, take this,' he said, embarrassed by her tears but thinking none the less, Pity that Jerry's here or I'd make a proper job of comforting her this time.

Major Trommel said coldly, 'To me it is perfectly clear what has happened. As the war has progressed northward through the country, the inhabitants of the mountains have reverted to their pre-war occupation, magnificently assisted by the enormous quantities of small-arms and ammunition parachuted to them by the Allies under the misguided impression that they were supplying partisan groups.'

'Pre-war occupation?' said Widdicombe.

Major Trommel said darkly, 'Brigandage.'

'Oh.' Widdicombe looked thoughtful. 'You mean . . .?'

'I mean that those mules will never be seen again. I mean that the oil has by now been sold on the black market. I mean that the muleteers, if not dead, will have joined the brigands and are even now making great *Schlucken* from their wine-flasks and gigantic peals of laughter as they toy with female so-called partisans.'

'Stop!' cried the Countess, distraught. 'You are a filthy lying pig. I would bring the priest to excommunicate you if only those communists had not shot him. You stink, you horrible Nazi excrement scraped from the disgusting sewers of a pork factory, you impotent, cowardly, cadging, treacherous, venal, sycophantic, scurvy, time-serving, shuffling mongrel, you goat-footed, pimping, dust-licking, scum-gobbling *fango*, you . . .'

Major Widdicombe said, 'I say, don't let's get to the point where we lose our tempers, what?'

The Countess drew in a huge breath and stared at him, dumbfounded for the moment.

'I mean, Major Trommel has a point there,' Widdicombe said reasonably. 'How d'you know that what he suggests hasn't in fact happened?'

The Countess raised her hands in the air and screamed, 'Because for twenty years the family has paid protection money to all the groups of brigands on the road, you cloth-headed, flop-eared, pot-bellied, flat-footed, short-winded . . .'

Widdicombe lost his own temper, touched on the raw by her choice of epithets. He barked, 'Shut up! That's quite enough.'

Before the Countess could answer, Widdicombe pointed to a chair.

'Sit down!' he snapped.

She hesitated, then suddenly melted, sitting obediently, her eyes soft and limpid.

'Ah!' she sighed. 'You are a masterful man. Beneath the velvet glove, the iron fist. I am sorry, Major.'

'Very well,' Widdicombe said, pleased and flattered. 'Now just you carry on calmly and quietly. How can you expect anyone to help you if you fly off the handle at them every two minutes?'

'True,' she said, and dabbed at her eyes with Widdicombe's large khaki handkerchief. Then she went on: 'The mules always come by mountain paths. It is a journey of perhaps four hundred kilometres in a straight line, but nearer seven or eight because the paths are very twisty, you know?'

'Five hundred miles at the outside,' Widdicombe said. 'Do you know if the mule train ever set out?'

'Oh yes,' the Countess said. 'Every year they take back with them a dozen pigeons from the dovecot. Every year one or two come back in the very early spring with the message. Only one pigeon came this year, but that was enough. The mule train is on its way, but where? My poor mules and my poor men—think of them, Major, think of the oil! Please help me: find my mules!'

Major Trommel said, 'It is quite out of the question. The mountains south of here are infested with brigands and with partisans of every conceivable political faction, all fighting one another. We cannot help you, Countess. You must promise not to start screaming at me again, and you must listen. Last year there were only your old bands of brigands: those to whom you paid the safe-conduct money. This year there are dozens of other groups, plus the partisans. Your mule train is in the middle of the fire, and I am not going to jump into the frying pan to get roasted. The decision is not Major Widdicombe's because he is my prisoner. Is that clear?'

His voice rose through the rattle and bang of the guns down in the plain.

'That is where you ought to be,' said the Countess icily. 'Down there, getting your turnip head shot off.'

Major Trommel went to the door, turning with one hand on the knob. He said, 'I have had enough insults for one day, and I have enough problems of my own to have given Bismarck a nervous breakdown. Now I am going to the command post to watch what is happening down there, and to think over a course of action.'

He bowed curtly, and left the room.

'Well,' said Major Widdicombe, 'I've often wondered how it would feel if I were ever taken prisoner.'

'And how do you feel?' the Countess asked.

'I feel just the same. At the time it was pretty rotten—you know, handing over to Trommel and all that—but it doesn't seem to have made all that much difference, except that I think about the men more: what'll happen to them and so on.'

The Countess said softly, 'Put it all out of your mind, dear Major,' and placed a hand on his arm. 'There are still a few little details to discuss. Come.'

She led him up the next flight of stairs to a large room with a painted ceiling and a huge bed, closing the door behind her and twisting the tiny catch in the centre of the handle, locking it. Major Widdicombe moistened his lips, looking at the ceiling.

'Is this your room?'

The Countess nodded and said, 'Call me Sismonda . . . William.'

Widdicombe frowned and said, 'I found Trommel wandering around in here last night.'

'Yes,' said the Countess distastefully, and spat on the floor. 'The pig is always sniffing and rootling after me. But I anticipated him, and last night I—I slept elsewhere. *Furba*, that is I: cunning.'

'I knew it!' Widdicombe said, excited. 'Why, the horrible man!'

'Do not disturb yourself,' the Countess said, coming close and kissing Widdicombe's ear, then nibbling the lobe. 'Tuk-tuk,' she said into his ear, and then stood back, her hands loosely on his shoulders. Major Widdicombe gave an incoherent growl and propelled her to the bed.

Some time later the Countess sat up, stretching and humming while Widdicombe gazed up at her with ashen adoration. She broke off and said dreamily, 'William Widdicombe? Villiam Viddicomba loves Sismonda?'

'My God, yes, Major Widdicombe said fervently.

She slapped him idly on the stomach and said, 'It was good?'

'Oof,' he said, the breath expelled from his body. 'Phew. I'd do anything for you . . . I say, though, you never—well, you never—hrrm, had—er'm . . .'

'What? What is it, my big darling, my great big strong?' she asked.

'Had-anything-to-do-with-that-fellow-Trommel?' Major Widdicombe said as fast as he could, hating the question but compelled to it.

The Countess rolled over and gripped Major Widdicombe by the hair above his ears, both fists clenching.

'Eek!' -

'I should bite off your nose,' she said intensely. 'Have I not said that I avoided him? Last night I slept in one of the *servants' rooms*,' she hissed. 'You think I am lying?'

'Ow!' Major Widdicombe said. ' 'Course not, Scout's honour I believe you, see it wet, see it dry.'

The Countess thought for a moment and then giggled, relaxing comfortably on top of him.

'What a funny expression,' she said. 'So *sottosopra*.'

Major Widdicombe breathed heavily inside an auburn fog of hair.

'What's that?'

'Upside down,' she murmured.

And eventually the Countess sat up again and said, 'It must be almost time for lunch.' She nudged him in the ribs. 'Lovers in books, in the romances I have read, they are never hungry; they pine and moon about, off their food. Nonsense! I could eat an elephant.'

'You're right, Sismonda. Odd, I'd never thought of it like that, but it's true . . . Steak. And eggs. And a bottle of stout,' he added enthusiastically.

'Eat while we can,' the Countess agreed, then leaned her elbows on her knees, gloom descending. 'Eat while we can: tomorrow comes the hangman.'

'I say, that's a bit morbid, isn't it?'

'Not for me,' she said. 'If that oil does not come by the end of the month, then the communists will say that the big capitalist has given orders for it to be sold on the way. It means nothing to them that I would gladly die for my villagers; the reds will have the excuse they have been waiting for. If the mules do not come by the end of the month, the communists will hang me, and I shall have died in vain.'

Major Widdicombe had shot bolt upright in the bed.

'You're joking!' he said incredulously.

'No, William.' She sighed, patting her hair absently. 'Now you know another reason why I want you to find my mules.'

'Good lord,' Widdicombe said, the background noise of guns suddenly turned to tumbrils and kettledrums. 'We must find them! But how? Trommel won't let me do anything. I'm a prisoner.'

'There is perhaps a way,' the Countess said. 'I will tell you my little plan while we dress.'

*   *   *

Major Trommel had spent a busy couple of hours getting up to date with the paperwork at the command post, filling in forms retrospectively, a small part of his brain worrying about Wohlhaber's strange behaviour. But when he reached the situation report for that day, Major Trommel's lips pursed with pride, and he forgot Wohlhaber as he recounted the events, striving to maintain the official phrasing while at the same time giving prominence to his own exemplary action in taking four British prisoners. Earlier he had omitted the unfortunate affair of the Tiger tank, but it was very much in his mind as he initialled the report and spiked it.

What was he to do? He thought, The correct course is to put those inconvenient witnesses to death. The *Genickschuss*. Wohlhaber brings them to the command post one by one, and as each comes past me he feels only a brief chill as the muzzle of my pistol touches his neck at the base of the skull; then oblivion. . . . No: *I* bring them in, and *Wohlhaber* . . .

He threw down his pencil on the desk. 'Weakling!' he said aloud. 'Disgrace to the Wehrmacht! The Countess is right, and I am a coward, afraid to be ruthless, a failure as a soldier, good for nothing but the *Genickschuss* myself.'

Major Trommel rose from his desk, resolved. He would march down alone into the plain, find a senior officer and give himself up, take his medicine like a man: the endless hours of Gestapo interrogation, the rubber truncheons, the castor oil, the electric treatment, the pincers. . . . He shuddered, hanging on to control of himself with heaven knew what reserves of courage, and made for the door, tears streaming down his cheeks. He marched on shaky legs into the square, heading for the road down into the plain.

*   *   *

Private Wohlhaber lay on his bed snoring heavily, catching up on his sleep after the previous night's exertions, dreaming not of the Countess—who had indeed slept in this veritable servant's room—but of eating a length of *Jagdwurst*, his mouth opened to its widest to accommodate the diameter of the sausage, the far end of which was growing while he ate. His mouth was working as he snored; the other end of the sausage swelled, monstrous features developing as he chewed and chewed.

At the foot of the bed stood the fat terra cotta vase containing the battered and dusty artificial flowers. The door opened, and Filomena peered round it, then came in on tiptoe. She went stealthily to the foot of the bed.

The sausage opened a mouth of scimitar teeth and sang,

> 'Regentropfen
> An meinem Fenster klopfen:
> Ich liebe Dich,'

as it clashed its teeth and grew larger, approaching Wohlhaber; he stirred in the bed, flinging out a hand and moaning. Swiftly Filomena picked up the vase and backed out of the room, closing the door quietly.

'The flowers,' she said, handing over the vase to the fat woman in black with a hiss of relief, and then they both hurried downstairs.

In the bedroom the sausage had grown a top hat and white tie and was singing,

> 'Komm, Herzens Liebchen! Lass uns gehn
> Da wo die Waldes Winde wehn:
> Da sagen wir Aufwiedersehn . . .'

and the huge tunnel of jaws opened into a wet red darkness engulfing Wohlhaber; he awoke gasping and shuddering. He staggered to the wash-stand in the corner of the spartan room and splashed cold water over his face.

*　　　*　　　*

Major Trommel paused at the head of the road, the tears drying on his cheeks. He looked back at the village, at the bulk of the palazzo overshadowing it, turned and gulped, then took out a handkerchief and blew his nose with a sudden trombone-effect. A small brown dog asleep in the shade of the parapet leaped to its feet, barking. Major Trommel thought, The condemned man's last wish: a cigarette, but I have none. Ah well . . . He straightened his shoulders and saluted the palazzo gravely in farewell, holding the pose, statuesque.

Private Dorbell appeared at the opposite side of the square, coming from the palazzo. He halted on seeing Trommel, and then saluted back, sloppily. He walked across the square to the major and said, 'You know, you didn't ought to salute me, being as you're an officer. I'm the one that ought to salute you. Any road, you're wanted.'

'Wanted? Why?'

'I don't know,' Dorbell said. 'I'm only a private.'

'Do you smoke? Have you any cigarettes?'

'No. I give my ration away. Are you coming, then?'

Major Trommel looked down into the plain where ants shot at one another, where toy tanks crawled and model aircraft buzzed in the air. He thought, At least I'll get a cigarette before I go.

'Yes,' he said. 'I'm coming.'

They walked to the palazzo, into the courtyard past the marble nymph and her stone fish, and into the kitchen. Major Widdicombe was seated at the table, in the centre of which stood the vase of artificial flowers. The Countess sat by his side, and behind them Sergeant Entwistle and Corporal White were standing. As his eyes grew used to the shadowy kitchen after the dazzle of sunlight, Major Trommel saw Filomena in the background with Gina, a fat woman in black, and a little girl.

'Oh, good, here you are,' Major Widdicome said pleasantly.

The inner door opened and Wohlhaber came in, his hair damp and frowsty, his eyes widening as he noticed the flowers.

'Now we can get on with it,' Widdicombe said, and the Countess spoke in Italian.

The fat woman came forward shoving the little girl in front of her, then leaned over and picked up the vase.

'Oh no!' said Major Trommel.

'Oh yes,' Widdicombe said, standing. 'The Allies have recaptured all ground lost. Now you and this chap of yours are my prisoners again.'

The little girl took the vase and handed it to Major Widdicombe, who said, 'Bless you, my dear,' and kissed the top of her head; Gina and Filomena cheered thinly. Major Widdicombe held out his hand to Trommel.

'Now I'll just have my gun back,' he said airily, and turned to Sergeant Entwistle. 'Catch.' He tossed the vase through the air.

Wohlhaber uttered a sudden shout as Entwistle fumbled, almost dropping the vase, but getting his other hand to it just in time.

'Butterfingers!' Corporal White said.

Major Widdicombe said, 'Now put those bloody flowers away somewhere, Sergeant.' He turned back to Trommel. 'The gun.'

Slowly Major Trommel took out Widdicombe's revolver and returned it to him.

'Have you a cigarette?' he asked.

'That all you've got to say?' Widdicombe asked, giving him a cigarette and lighting it.

Major Trommel inhaled the smoke deeply, blew it out again and looked down at Widdicombe.

'No,' he said. 'Not quite all. You have just saved my life.'

'Eh?'

'No matter,' said Trommel. 'I am in your hands, Major.'

'That's fine,' Widdicombe told him. 'You and that man of yours had better get your kit into marching order. We leave at dusk this evening.'

The Countess smiled beatifically while Trommel stared in mystification.

'What are you looking so happy about?' he said.

Major Widdicombe beamed, 'We are going in search of the mules. Now let's go upstairs and have a drink, eh? Lunch doesn't seem nearly ready yet; all this fuss and bother's made it late.'

'I will have a drink with the greatest of pleasure,' Trommel said. 'But if you think I am going on a wild-duck chase with you, then you are barking up the wrong end of the stick.'

'Come on,' Widdicombe said firmly. 'We'll have a drink and talk it over. Remember you're my prisoner again now. . . . Coming, Countess?'

8

MAJOR WIDDICOMBE opened his last bottle of whisky, pouring small drinks for the Countess and himself, and a very large one for Major Trommel.

'Cheers.'

Major Trommel looked dubiously at his glass; the Countess smiled at him and raised hers to him. He sipped tentatively, then drank the rest of the whisky at once.

'Have another spot,' Widdicombe said encouragingly.

Trommel held out his glass and said, 'This is all very well but I am not going with you to look for those mules. I am your prisoner and willing to give parole, but you cannot compel me to . . .'

'Compel?' said Major Widdicombe. 'My dear fellow, perish the thought.'

'No compulsion,' the Countess agreed.

Major Widdicombe swished the whisky round in his glass and sipped.

'Then what can you say?' asked Trommel. 'You want me to go; I do not want to go; and yet you say you will not compel me.'

Widdicombe said, 'I'm appealing to your sense of chivalry, first of all. The Countess informs me that she is under sentence of execution if these mules do not arrive at Borgo San Marco by the end of the month, and she has a letter to prove it.'

He signed to the Countess, who passed him a letter which he handed in turn to Major Trommel.

Respected Countess,

We, the People's Tribunal of the Commune of Borgo San Marco, wish to direct your notice to the following resolution, which was passed nemine contradicente *at the last meeting of the Tribunal:*

'Whereas Sismonda Giulietta Maria Francesca, Countess of San Marco, stands suspect as a lackey of the effete imperialist powers by reason of her irresponsible actions towards those tenants and others whose faces have been persistently ground into the dust, deprived of the necessities of life, subjected to extortion and humiliation, degraded by the non-fulfilment of her duties towards them—this Tribunal resolves that should the long-awaited and presumably previously disposed-of consignment of oil fail to arrive by the expiration of the current month, thereby providing conclusive proof of her criminality, she shall be summarily and publicly executed in the Piazza Garibaldi, which to signalise the joyful occasion shall thenceforth be known as the Piazza Stalino.'

The Red Flag shall triumph! Long live communism and the liberty of the people!

Assuring your Ladyship of our respectful obedience at all times,

Renzo Martello

'Jolly sinister, I call it,' Major Widdicombe said as Trommel finished reading. 'I mean, we can't just stand by and let these chaps hang Sismonda, can we?'

'Ha,' Major Trommel said. 'Sismonda now, is it? We have become on good terms all of a sudden, have we not?'

The Countess said, 'Of course I allow William to use my first name. He has proved a friend, and so is entitled to the little marks of affection which go with friendship.'

'Little marks of affection!' Trommel snorted. 'And all I have is the scars.'

'Look,' Widdicombe said, 'you've seen that letter. These chaps mean business. We can't just stand and do nothing while they take justice into their own hands like that.'

'Take it into your own hands,' Trommel shrugged. '*You* hang *them*.'

The Countess said, 'They have gone underground, and no one knows where they are or how to find them.' She turned to Major Widdicombe. 'It is no use arguing this way with Major Trommel. He requires logical proof of the necessity of finding the mules. . . . Is that not so, Major Trommel?'

Trommel nodded.

'Absolutely,' he said. 'We are a logical race, we Germans.'

'Come then,' she said to him, and to Widdicombe: 'This would bore you. Bear with me for a little while. I can see that I shall have to apply all the force of argument at my disposal to convince Major Trommel that I am worth saving. We shall not be long.'

She led Major Trommel to an inner door; it closed behind them and Major Widdicombe was left in some puzzlement. Eventually he shrugged and drank the rest of his whisky, a little hurt, and thinking, Damn it all, does she think I can't argue logically if I have to? Well, perhaps she's right as far as these German johnnies are concerned. . . . Better make a list of what we've got to take with us. Toothpaste first; mustn't forget the old dentifrice.

He pulled out notebook and pencil, and soon became immersed, starting with surprise when at length the door opened and the Countess came in. Major Widdicombe glanced at his watch.

'Good heavens!' he said. 'You've been gone three-quarters of an hour.'

'Yes,' said the Countess, while Widdicombe noticed that her face was quite flushed with the exertion of argument. 'It took longer than I had estimated.'

Major Trommel entered, giving a little skip across the threshold, and the Countess said to him, 'But at least I have convinced you that I am worth saving?'

'Oh yes,' Major Trommel said emphatically. 'I am completely convinced. You have resolved all my doubts.'

'How did you manage it?' Widdicombe asked the Countess.

She said casually, 'I put it to him, pro against con, item against item, Italian subtlety against German stiffness. It was by no means easy going, but as you see, I had the victory. It was not for nothing that my race produced Boccaccio and Aretino,' she added with pride.

'Oh yes, of course,' Major Widdicombe said, out of his depth. 'Jolly deep thinkers those chaps, I always say. My word, I *am* pleased, though!—Tell you what, we'll have another drink, just to celebrate, and then we'll go to lunch, eh?'

He poured drinks for the three of them, and they clinked glasses, toasting one another, each eminently satisfied.

9

6 'WOHLHABER. Where is Wohlhaber?' said Major Trommel. 'I sent him to fetch my greatcoat and the dolt has been away twenty minutes already.'

The search party stood outside the palazzo in full marching order, carrying in their packs loads which increased in weight with decrease in rank, Private Dorbell almost invisible beneath the bulk of his accoutrements and impedimenta. Already tired, he had leaned back against the wall. Major Widdicombe wore khaki drill slacks and a battle-dress jacket, haversack and sidearms, binoculars slung round his neck, and he felt rather dashing as he tapped his swagger stick against his thigh.

Sergeant Entwistle said, 'Dusk ain't yet: the sun's still up. Dusk, you said, sir.'

Widdicombe said testily, 'I said we were to move at dusk. Surely you can see that means we must be ready beforehand?'

Major Trommel said, 'I must apologise for Wohlhaber. I cannot think what could be causing the delay.'

The Countess appeared at an upper window of the palazzo, smiling, waving and blowing kisses.

'Are you all ready?' she called.

'All except for Wohlhaber,' Widdicombe shouted.

'Here he is,' Corporal White said, as Wohlhaber suddenly came into view in the archway, carrying Major Trommel's greatcoat and panting. In addition to the pack on his back he was carrying two Schmeisser machine-pistols, a belt holding four stick grenades, and an entrenching tool.

'*Achtung!*' said Major Trommel. '*Stillgestanden!*'

Wohlhaber snapped to attention, and Major Trommel circled round him, inspecting his kit.

'Gor!' said Corporal White to Sergeant Entwistle. 'Talk about bull . . .'

Above the perennial sound of distant gunfire they heard a wasp-like buzz increasing in intensity, and simultaneously a group of villagers ran up the street from the square, shouting in panic. Gina and Filomena dashed from the rear entrance of the palazzo and began to tug at Sergeant Entwistle and Corporal White, sobbing and screeching.

From above the Countess yelled, 'Hurry, hurry! Soldiers are coming on motor-cycles! Hurry, or you will all be killed!'

'Dusk or no bloody dusk,' Sergeant Entwistle said, 'I've got a feeling it's time we weren't here.'

Major Widdicombe said, 'You're dead right. I'll lead, then Major Trommel, then you, Sergeant. After you I want that chap Wohlhaber, then Corporal White; Dorbell at the rear. Understood?'

They shuffled into position while the women and villagers shouted and gave conflicting advice in incomprehensible dialect.

'Right, off we go: at the double!'

'Goodbye!' the Countess shouted. 'I will get rid of the soldiers. Hurry now, and find my mules!'

They began to move off.

'Cheerio, Sismonda,' Widdicombe called.

'Till we meet again, Sismonda,' called Trommel.

'Always at your command, Countess,' Wohlhaber called.

'Help!' said another voice. 'I'm stook.'

'Hurry: the soldiers are coming!' the Countess squeaked from her point of vantage.

Dorbell panted and heaved, fixed immovably to the wall by the weight of his kit; Entwistle and White rushed back and hauled him upright, dragging him after the others. Widdicombe paused for a final wave to the Countess, and then they were round the corner and in a narrow alley strung with lines of washing. They tore shirts and camisoles and trousers from their faces and hurried on; the buzz of motor-cycles had become a roar; and as the party came to the end of the alley and clattered across a weedy paved space dotted with a few skeletal, doomed-looking chickens, the engine noise spluttered into silence. The paving ended in a straggling edging of thyme, then they found a gap from which led a narrow path through bushes and cypresses. They ran in single file until Major Widdicombe was out of breath, and he halted them with an upraised hand. Dorbell was bent over so far that he did not see the signal, cannoning into Corporal White, who cursed.

'Ssh!' said Major Widdicombe.

Snorts of heavy breathing; a dog barking in the village; the rumble of guns far away; nothing else. Major Widdicombe felt the westering sun warm on his forehead, inhaled the scent of aromatic leaves crushed underfoot, heard the sudden ticking of some insect in the brushwood, and relaxed as he regained his breath.

'Path leads upwards now,' he said. 'Take it slowly. No talking and no smoking. Come on.'

They forged on, turning and climbing with the path, the sun hidden now by a black spur of rock before them. Still they climbed and turned, high above the village and to westward of it; the vegetation became sparser; and at length Major Widdicombe called another halt. They dropped exhausted on to a flat outcrop of rock, Private Dorbell lying on his back on the mound of kit, an up-ended turtle. Major Widdicombe gazed through his binoculars at the village, focussing on the expanse of ground before the palazzo. As he adjusted the focus, the two blurred circles of bright light merged into one, acquiring definition.

'Well?' said Major Trommel.

'I can see two motor-cycle combinations outside the palazzo. Nobody in sight. . . . Oh, yes now I see them. They're in the shade. Four of them—no, six. Talking to the Countess. Or she's talking to them, rather: she's waving her arms and I can see her mouth opening and shutting.'

'And the soldiers?' Major Trommel asked.

'They're just standing there. Listening. I suppose. My word, she's certainly giving them what for!'

Major Widdicombe lowered the binoculars, cackling falsely. Trommel studied him, then held out a hand.

'The soldiers,' he said.

Resignedly Widdicombe passed over the binoculars, while Major Trommel focussed them and said, 'I thought so. British troops do not use motor-cycle combinations. They are German soldiers.'

'Well, yes . . .'

'There has been no battle,' Trommel said. 'How could there be German soldiers at the village if the British hold the plain? I do not understand.'

Widdicombe made a noncommital gesture and said, 'Situation's very confused. Never know what's happening. . . .'

His voice trailed off under Major Trommel's indignant glare.

'Perfidious Albion, you have tricked me,' Trommel said.

Furiously he scrambled to his feet, cupping his hands to his mouth preparatory to yelling for help. Sergeant Entwistle rose also and hit Major Trommel neatly on the point of the chin; Corporal White caught him under the upper arms as he sagged, and lowered him to the floor.

'Thank you,' said Major Widdicombe in surprise. 'That was very nicely done.'

He signed to Wohlhaber, who loosened Major Trommel's collar and began to fan him with his cap. After a few moments Trommel stirred, opening his eyes. Then he sat up groggily. Major Widdicombe was gazing through the binoculars once more.

Trommel said, 'Swine! That was not fair play.'

He rubbed his chin, looking as though he might burst into tears.

'Dirty filthy English swine,' he said defiantly.

'Now you shut your cakehole, mate,' Sergeant Entwistle said pleasantly, 'or you'll get one stuck on you as'll lay you out for a fortnight.'

Major Trommel sniffed.

Widdicombe lowered the binoculars and said, 'They've gone. They're off back where they came from, thank goodness.' He stood and looked down at Major Trommel. 'You're a silly ass, aren't you? What d'you think those blokes were up to? I'll bet you a solid brass battleship they'd come to ask questions about your precious Tiger tank. What would have happened if you'd yelled out just then? They'd have taken me and my men prisoner, but what would they have done to you? I thought we'd had all that out already.'

Major Trommel considered, licked his lips nervously and said, 'Of course, you are right. I had forgotten because I was angry with you. I apologise.'

'Very handsome. Now let's get some sleep and be up at

the crack of dawn. And then we'll start looking for those mules.' Widdicombe called to Dorbell, 'Find my sleeping bag, Dorbell, and blow up my air mattress.'

'One thing, Major,' Trommel said, looking round in the gathering twilight.'

'What's that?'

'If the German troops still hold the plain east of here, then the situation is as it was.'

'What do you mean?'

'You are my prisoners,' Major Trommel said. 'And tomorrow *I* shall lead the way.'

'Oh, bloody hell,' said Major Widdicombe.

And Corporal White said to Private Dorbell, who was hunting through the mound of kit, 'I tell you what, Knocker. You don't have to go *looking* for mules. We've got two of the bleeders here.'

*   *   *

They passed a restless night, with the exception of Major Widdicombe, who was comfortably insulated from protruding rocks by his air mattress, which his mother had given him as a present after his embarkation leave. Punctually at six o'clock he awoke, sat up and stretched, yawning, and then woke the others, ordering Dorbell and Corporal White to serve cold corned beef and biscuits.

'Can't make a fire yet,' he said. 'We might be seen.'

Major Trommel groaned and rose stiffly from the ground, still draped in a single blanket over his greatcoat. He began rubbing at sore spots and aching joints.

'What a night!' he said. 'It was terrible. In future we must choose our sleeping place with proper care.'

'What d'you mean by that?' Major Widdicombe demanded huffily. 'What's wrong with this place? I spent a perfectly comfortable night here.'

'Yes, Major,' said Trommel, 'but we have not all one of those obscene airbeds. I ache in every piece of my body as though I had been pulled through a mangle backwards.'

'Obscene?'

'Every time you turned over, that thing made a vulgar noise,' Major Trommel said. '*Prrrp*. So. I could not sleep because of it.'

They munched the corned beef and biscuits, washed down with water from their bottles.

'Shai,' said Sergeant Entwistle. 'That's what I need: a good mug of shai to lay this horrible food.'

White nodded in agreement, while Private Dorbell finished serving himself and sat down apart.

'Fwot we are about tweet,' he said aloud, 'may the Lord make us truly thankful,' and he nibbled despondently at the edge of his biscuit.

'What's up, Knocker?' Corporal White said. 'Cheesed off already?'

Private Dorbell looked up and said, 'I'm lornly.'

'Lonely?'

'It's like this,' Dorbell said. 'There's two officers, and two N.C.O.s and then me.'

Corporal White jerked a thumb at Wohlhaber, who was gobbling hungrily.

'What about 'im, then?'

'Well, I can't count him, can I? He doesn't talk English, and I can't talk German. What's the use of that? I still feel lornly. And I'm a prisoner again. I don't like being a prisoner, Corp. I keep on thinking they'll take us off to Germany and make us have nowt but sausages and beer.'

Sergeant Entwistle said, 'Sausages and beer, kwais ketir, I wish I had some now instead of this muck. Don't you worry, Dorbell.'

White said, 'He's right, Knocker: it doesn't matter a monkey's continental which of us lot's prisoners and which isn't. It's the blind leading the blind all the way.'

Major Widdicombe finished his breakfast and took out his cigarette case, considered and said, 'On second thoughts, perhaps not. Better not smoke yet.' He called to Dorbell, 'Pack away now, will you? We'll move in five minutes.'

'Excuse me, I am in charge now,' said Major Trommel.

'Oh, hell. I was forgetting. So you are,' Widdicombe said in chagrin.

'So we move in *six* minutes,' said Trommel self-importantly. 'I will lead, and Private Wohlhaber will bring up the rear this time.'

Widdicombe smirked. 'How do you know which way to go? You don't know the way, do you?'

Major Trommel was taken aback.

'Why . . .' he said. '. . . Er, that way,' and pointed along the path.

'Ah, yes, but when the path forks? Good heavens, man, it's a proper maze of paths. Still, don't let me influence you,' Widdicombe said nastily. 'Carry on—lead us right to the German lines, or the British, whichever you prefer. Of course, I'm only a prisoner now, but I happen to have a map.'

'Ha,' said Trommel. 'A map! So: I will confiscate it.'

'And I'll knock your head off if you try,' Sergeant Entwistle told him.

Major Trommel bit his lip in thought.

'We are in an impasse,' he said. 'Up the backside of a sack. But perhaps a compromise is possible. Major Widdicombe shall have the status and title of guide.'

Widdicombe perked up.

'Guide?' he said. 'That sounds all right to me. Yes, I rather fancy that. Very well.' He opened his battledress jacket and drew out a folded sheet of thick paper. 'There's the map, see.'

Major Trommel held out a hand, but Widdicombe forestalled him by snatching the map away.

'Not so fast,' he said. 'I'll hang on to this. You lead, but I'll tell you where to go. Everybody ready? Right then: straight on, Major . . .'

*   *   *

There was no way of telling whether the map was correct. Its basis was a cheap pre-war motoring map of Italy, on which the Countess had drawn the route taken by the annual mule train, a wavering vein of purple ink traced along the country's spine. It led round the shoulders of the hills, keeping as closely as possible for the first ten miles between the six-hundred- and eight-hundred-foot contours. The party saw no villages that morning, and no sign of life; the path twisted endlessly among the hills, here and there subdividing, here and there an offshoot leading downward until it disappeared among scrub and woodland. At one o'clock Major Trommel called the noon halt, and this time Private Dorbell and Private Wohlhaber gathered twigs for a fire so that tea could be brewed and hot food prepared: dehydrated potato and egg, together with the left-over corned beef from breakfast. They all made faces at the thought, but all ate like starving gannets. Major Widdicombe rubbed his feet absently, having removed his shoes, and was surprised to find that he had no blisters.

Major Trommel said, 'Water. We must find some water during the afternoon. The water bottles are almost empty, and we shall use more in washing out our canteens.'

'Canteens?' Widdicombe looked puzzled. 'Oh, you mean mess-tins. Yes, I suppose we must find some water.

Sismonda didn't mention where we could get it.' He gazed at the hills, the stands of forest, the scrubland, the cypresses spiking the lower slopes, and said, 'Doesn't seem to be much water about, somehow.'

They trudged on throughout the afternoon, heading in a generally southerly direction, the sun moving round from their faces to their right cheeks, and at four o'clock Corporal White said to Widdicombe, 'Look, sir—down there.'

Widdicombe peered down into a deep valley, past over-grown terraces which betrayed that vines had once been cultivated there, to a small white building with a ruined roof of bright red tiles. He lifted his binoculars and scanned the building.

'Place is just a ruin,' he said. 'It must have been a farm-house once.'

'That's what I meant, sir,' Corporal White said. 'If it was a farmhouse, there must have been a spring or something.'

'By God, you're right: there is. Not a spring, though. It's a well.'

Major Widdicombe inspected it closely. The roof had gone, and there was something white draped on and over the coping.

'Left some of their washing when they moved out,' he said.

Major Trommel said, 'If there is a well, perhaps there is water in it still. We will go down and see.'

They clambered and slithered down the slope to the building. All four walls still stood, but the windows were broken and the door had been half torn from its hinges. Dorbell and Wohlhaber wandered inside, driven by the universal desire of people to ferret about in abandoned habitations; the others walked to the well, seeing that the white material draped from the coping was of silk: the upper portion of a parachute. Major Widdicombe peered into the depths of the well.

'Good lord,' he said. 'The view's completely blocked. I can't see if there's any water or not. There's a chap down there.' He called into the well, his voice hollowly amplified, 'I say, you down there. Are you all right?'

The figure which was hanging from the parachute harness stirred, and a dim white face looked up.

'I'd gone clean off to sleep,' it said. 'Haul me up now, hey?'

'Right you are,' said Major Widdicombe. 'You didn't by any chance notice if there's any water down there, I suppose?'

'There sure is,' said the parachutist. 'Too much for my liking. Now will you for Chrissakes get me out of here?'

Major Widdicombe turned from the well.

'Where the devil has Dorbell got to?' he asked petulantly. 'And that fellow Wohlhaber.'

'In there, sir,' Sergeant Entwistle told him, pointing to the house.

'Corporal White, go and fetch those two at the double.'

'Yes, sir.'

White disappeared into the house, and found Dorbell inspecting a German water bottle which lay on the bare floor, while Wohlhaber squatted in a corner, resting.

'Come on,' White said. 'You're wanted at the double.'

Private Dorbell said, 'That's a Jerry water bottle, that is. I want it for a souvenir.'

'You leave it alone,' White shouted. 'Come on, get moving, both of you.'

Dorbell and Wohlhaber looked at each other; Dorbell gestured to the doorway. Each shrugged with resignation, then moved out very slowly, followed by Corporal White.

'Come on,' Major Widdicombe yelled. 'Double over here.'

Groans and curses reverberated in the well. Interested, Dorbell and Wohlhaber increased their pace, reached the well and leaned on the coping looking down.

'Eee,' said Private Dorbell. 'What's that man doing down there?'

'Dorbell!' roared Major Widdicombe.

'Wohlhaber!' roared Major Trommel.

'Pull him out!' they roared together.

Dorbell and Wohlhaber sighed and leaned down, lifting the loose part of the parachute canopy out of the way and grasping the suspension lines.

'Don't tell me,' the parachutist said. 'Somebody's finally going to help me.'

Dorbell and Wohlhaber hauled and grunted, but could not budge the load.

'It's no use,' Dorbell said, panting. 'He's too heavy.'

Major Widdicombe signed to Entwistle and White. They joined the two private soldiers, and then foot by foot the parachutist was pulled from the well.

'Little Tommy Stout, I presume?' he said to Dorbell, getting both elbows on the coping, then a knee, and finally rolling over to an upright position, while at the same time he snapped off the parachute release and shrugged off the harness. Then he looked at the others, his glance flashing back to Trommel and Wohlhaber.

'Krauts,' he said. 'Two Krauts!'

Major Trommel stiffened, glaring icily at the tall, capless figure in stained and dusty U.S. Army uniform; the man's blond hair was tousled and his grey eyes bleared by strain and sleep.

'I am an officer of the Wehrmacht,' Trommel said. 'These British are my prisoners, and so are you.'

'Whad he say?' The parachutist looked in amazement at Major Widdicombe. 'Prisoners?'

' 'Fraid so,' said Widdicombe. 'First of all *we* took *them* prisoner, and then. . . . Well, it's rather a long story, but we've changed over a few times, actually. Shouldn't worry if I were you, old man.'

The American sat down on the coping of the well and scratched his head in bewilderment. Dorbell and Wohlhaber were starting a fire beside the wall of the house.

'That's right,' Major Widdicombe said. 'You sit down while we make some tea. My name's Widdicombe. He's Trommel.'

'Major Trommel,' the German said.

'Quite. Major Widdicombe as well. That other Jerr— I mean German, that's Trommel's servant. The others are my chaps. Who are you?'

'Spud Henryson. Lieutenant. I'm from Wichita, Kansas. My real given name's Stanford, but most everybody calls me Spud.'

'I hope you won't think me inquisitive,' Widdicombe said, 'but would you mind telling me how you got down that well?'

'Sure,' said Henryson. 'I baled out of a B.17 early this morning. I wasn't part of the crew or anything: just flew out from Tunis for the ride. We hit heavy anti-aircraft fire up north and the captain made me jump.'

'What about the others?'

Henryson looked glum and said, 'They stayed with the ship to try and take her to some airfield. I felt a heel, but that captain had a gun in his hand and he wasn't about to listen to arguments. "Jump, buster," he said. "I never seen you aboard this plane and maybe I'll never see you again, but jump." So I jumped. It's a big crime, taking unauthorised personnel along on a mission. Everybody does it, but it means loss of seniority for the captain if he's caught. That captain sure loved his seniority more than he loved me.'

'And you landed down the well?'

'Right,' said Henryson. 'It's a hell of a way back to Tunis. I aim to head back north and bum a ride as soon as I locate an airfield.'

'Lucky we found you in a way,' said Widdicombe thoughtfully.

'Yeh. I might have died down there.'

'No,' Widdicombe told him, 'that's not what I meant. That water's a long way down, and we shouldn't have been able to reach it. But now we can fill our bottles easily by tying them to lengths of cord from that parachute.'

Henryson gaped, then said, 'Help yourself, Major.'

Widdicombe ordered the sergeant and the corporal to cut up lengths of parachute cord and then refill the water bottles, while Major Trommel handed Henryson a mug of tea.

'There,' he said. 'Soon we shall have biscuits and jam. English afternoon tea, you understand. I am dependent on my prisoners for my food supplies.'

'And everything else,' Widdicombe said indignantly. 'What about the map?'

'Map?' said Henryson, looking up sharply over the rim of his mug. 'What is all this? You guys after buried treasure or something?'

'No, not treasure. At least, not buried treasure,' Major Trommel said. 'We have a mission.'

'Like what?'

Trommel glanced at Widdicombe, who said, 'I think we can be frank.'

'Well,' said Trommel, 'we are searching for a mule

train. At least, we have only just begun, but a mule train is our ultimate objective.'

Henryson said, 'You're kidding, of course. Two Germans and four Britishers in the middle of nowhere, with a war on, looking for a mule train. Now tell me another.'

'Major Trommel is not kidding,' Widdicombe said. 'He is telling you the truth.'

'You're four against two, you crazy Limey: why don't you take over? They got to sleep some time.'

Major Widdicombe said, 'I can see you haven't got the point at all. If we did take over, we should still search for the mules.'

Henryson sighed and said, 'I'm still down the well, that's what it is. I'm asleep and now I'm dreaming some cockeyed dream full of crazy Krauts and Limeys, but in a minute I'll wake up for sure, and they'll be gone.'

Sergeant Entwistle, carrying a tin plate of sandwiches, joined the officers just as Major Trommel went close to Henryson and snapped his fingers under the man's nose, flicking it with his thumb.

'Ouch!' said Henryson, his eyes watering.

'Did you dream that?' Major Trommel inquired.

'Why, you lousy bastard.'

Henryson stood up and drew back his fist. Sergeant Entwistle put down the sandwich plate carefully on the coping of the well and said, 'I wouldn't if I was you, mate.'

Corporal White came up and stood behind Entwistle as Henryson stared at him. The sergeant was as tall as the American and a good deal heavier, his broad flat face set belligerently. It had that indefinably battered look which told a tale of street punch-ups and closing-time brawls.

'He's a German, and you're sticking up for him,' Henryson said, dropping his fist in amazement. 'Just look at him. A little old bald bag of bones.'

Corporal White said, 'He's a proper daredevil, is Major Trommel, a proper bloody daredevil. Why, I seen him knock a tank out single-handed. And *my* officer shot a plane down with a bloody pistol he did.'

'It wasn't a B.17?' Henryson said sarcastically, though obviously shaken.

'No, it was a Kitt . . .' Major Widdicombe began, but Major Trommel cut him off short, ganging up instinctively.

'A Stuka,' he said firmly. 'Now we will eat, and then move on until dark.'

Henryson subsided, taking a jam sandwich, while Widdicombe and Trommel exchanged satisfied glances.

*   *   *

They moved off at half past five, picking their way up the hillside towards the path. After fifty yards or so Major Widdicombe turned and looked idly back. He noticed that the fire was still burning, and said to Private Dorbell, 'Idiot, you haven't put out the fire. Never leave a fire burning. Go back and put it out now.'

Dorbell peered from beneath his mass of impedimenta and said, 'Oh, heck.'

'Go on at once. We'll wait here.'

Dorbell shed his kit and began to scramble down again; the others watched as he scattered the embers of the fire, rather perfunctorily. Then he hurried inside the building, and reappeared holding something. He trotted up to rejoin the rest of the party, calling, 'It's a good job I went back. I was forgetting me souvenir.'

He held up the German water bottle in triumph, gasping for breath.

'It's heavy,' he said.

'You and your blasted souvenirs,' Widdicombe grumbled. 'You didn't even put out that fire properly: it's still burning.'

Wohlhaber said suddenly in German, 'Let me see that,' and grabbed the bottle. He paled, then hurled the thing away from him.

'Me souvenir!' Dorbell wailed.

The bottle spun through the air, landed on the threshold of the house, and exploded deafeningly; immediately everyone was lying on the ground with arms over heads as wood and bricks and tiles fell all around. Then silence. They got to their feet and saw a cloud of dust rolling up-hill towards them.

'Booby-trap,' said Major Trommel succinctly.

Lieutenant Henryson gazed through the dust at the mass of debris beyond.

'It's gone out now,' he said. 'But that's a hell of a way to put out a fire.'

10

THANKS to Lieutenant Spud Henryson, the morale of the expedition was now high. Major Widdicombe and Major Trommel were united in determination to find the mule train, their national feelings submerged. Trommel in particular had been touched and gratified by Sergeant Entwistle and Corporal White's unexpected support, and both he and Widdicombe strode along happily.

'You saved me life,' Private Dorbell said to Private Wohlhaber. 'I don't feel lornly any more.'

Henryson walked along silently behind Major Widdicombe, his pleasant face puzzled. At length he hurried up to Widdicombe and grasped his arm.

'Look, you can level with me,' he said. 'All that crud about a mule train! You're in on some kind of racket: you must be.'

Major Widdicombe looked at him with a hint of impatience and said, 'My dear good chap, you're quite mistaken. We're looking for these mules because the village needs them. That's Borgo San Marco—the village where we happened to be. Sort of—er'm, well, a local relief project.'

Henryson said, 'You're both too good to be true. I know what you are. Secret Service, I bet: you don't fool me with all that "Ay say, may good chep". I just bet you're all in M.I.5.'

Widdicombe shrugged.

'You must have a naturally suspicious mind. But as a matter of fact there is a bit more to it, though not what you think. The life of a lady depends on our finding those mules,' he said portentously. 'She's my fiancée, if you must know.'

'You don't say?'

'I certainly do. The communists are going to execute her if we don't find those mules and take them back to Borgo San Marco.'

'In a pig's ear,' Henryson said, and left Widdicombe wondering what that meant. The American caught up Major Trommel, who was forging onward by himself, the daredevil leader of the expedition.

'What do you want?' he asked as Henryson drew level.

'I want to know what your racket is. I don't believe all that crap about finding a mule train.'

Major Trommel looked at Henryson coldly.

'You are at liberty to believe it or disbelieve it as you wish,' he said. 'Your opinions are of no possible interest to me, except in so far as I find you doubting my word. But you are a mere lieutenant, and I am a major of the Wehrmacht. Furthermore,' he added importantly, 'I am engaged to be married to a countess: a lady of noble blood, you understand. Her life depends on the success of our mission. If it should fail, the communist partisans will put her to death. That is an argument which convinces me; if it does not convince you, that is your affair. Now please to fall back into line. I have nothing further to say to you.'

Henryson lagged behind until Major Widdicombe came up to him. He said, 'Major. . . . This fiancée of yours. Who is she?'

Widdicombe said stiffly, 'I don't really know that it's any business of yours. I've got a feeling you were trying to be rude to me just then. If you don't like our company, please feel free to leave it. After all, we've only saved your life.'

'I'm sorry, Major.'

'Well, if you must know, she's a countess,' Widdicombe told him with some pride. 'Italian, of course, but right out of the top drawer, you can tell by the way she spits on the floor. I'm very fond of her. Dear old Sismonda,' he sighed. 'Swear I'm beginning to miss her already.'

'You know what?' Henryson said. 'I don't think you guys are British Intelligence at all. I think you're German Secret Service, the whole goddam shoot. You're just playing me along till we hit your headquarters and then you'll work me over.'

They were breasting a slope beyond which the path vanished into a copse of beech and scrub-oak. Henryson was licking his lips, pale, his eyes darting about as though looking for a way of escape.

'You're overwrought, old boy,' Major Widdicombe told him. 'Hang on a bit longer if you can. We'll be stopping for the night soon, and then you can get a good sleep. Amazing what a good rest can do. Why, if I'd jumped out of an aeroplane and landed down a well, I'm sure I'd be half crackers too, so cheer up.'

Henryson glanced over his shoulder, down to where Dorbell and Wohlhaber were walking companionably together. Wohlhaber was carrying Major Widdicombe's bedroll, while Dorbell had relieved him of the two Schmeissers.

'Get that,' Henryson said darkly. 'A British soldier carrying two German tommy-guns! I even saw that Kraut hand them over, and you're supposed to be prisoners! What kind of crazy set-up is this, when an escort gives a prisoner his guns to tote?'

Major Widdicombe sighed and said, 'It's no use talking to you, I can see that. A jolly good sleep, that's what you need.'

They walked among the trees, the path a scuffed rut in the leaf-mould. Ah, Sismonda, Widdicombe was thinking. Soon I'll be back with you in triumph with the mules, and you will marry me, and Good God, expect I'll become a sort of count or something. Henryson was scowling, between fear and truculence. He turned to say something to Major Widdicombe, but stopped at once, all motion frozen.

He said bitterly, 'You bastards. So this is the killing-ground.'

'What?'

Trommel glanced round and retraced his steps as Widdicombe held up a hand to halt the rest of the party.

Widdicombe said to him, 'Look here, Major, this fellow's all in. He's practically raving. I vote we stay here for the night and camp under the trees. All this leaf-mould'll be nice and comfy.'

Sergeant Entwistle came up and said, 'Good idea, sir.'

Henryson shuddered.

'This ain't a dream,' he said. 'It's a nightmare. There's a man behind every tree, just about.'

'See what I mean?' Widdicombe said to Major Trommel. 'He's shot to pieces.'

Major Trommel followed the direction of Henryson's gaze, stiffened, and said, 'That is what we shall be. Look.'

They looked, and for the first time saw the still figures behind the trees: men clad in rags and tatters of uniform, red scarves round their necks, red stars of cloth roughly sewn on their caps. They held a weird assortment of weapons—Short Model Lee Enfields, Schmeissers, Ross rifles, Lügers, Colts, Mausers. Bearded and swarthy, fierce and menacing, they moved forward in unison as one of them made a signal, waving a revolver.

Major Widdicombe dropped his swagger stick and said faintly, 'Better put down our guns.' He unbuckled his service belt, dropping it with holster and revolver to the ground. The others grounded their weapons also, then waited as the leader of the silent men reached the officers.

He was a small man with a thick black beard, little blood-shot eyes, and an unpleasant sneer which revealed a lot of bad teeth. He poked Major Trommel in the stomach with the muzzle of his revolver; Trommel gasped with pain and fear.

'A fascist pig,' the man said, and spat in Major Trommel's face. Trommel wiped away the spittle as the man turned to Major Widdicombe and Lieutenant Henryson. 'And a pair of capitalist jackals.'

The man jerked Widdicombe's binoculars over his head by their thong and began to put them on. Wohlhaber placed his entrenching tool on top of the stick grenades, then straightened up and walked casually over to Major Trommel.

'Communist partisans,' he said in German.

The leader swung at Wohlhaber back-handed, sending him staggering with blood running from his mouth. The other partisans—thirty or forty of them—had surrounded the little group.

'Now keep still,' the leader said. 'You are my prisoners. I am Renzo Martello; not that it will interest you beyond tomorrow.' He laughed nastily.

The other partisans jeered at their captives, then picked up the captured weapons, shouting remarks which were in some tortured dialect but which sounded threatening enough just the same.

Lieutenant Henryson said to Widdicombe, 'Sorry I said what I did. I'm . . .'

'Be silent!' Martello yelled. 'I am taking you garbage to our camp. You may have the night to make peace with your dirty capitalist God, and at dawn we shall shoot the lot of you.'

Private Dorbell said indignantly, 'You didn't ought to talk like that about God.'

Martello strode over to him and glowered at him.

He said, 'Snivelling lickspittle. Crawling lackey.'

Private Dorbell said with defiance, 'Sticks and storns may break my borns, but hard words cannot hurt me.'

'You shall have the sticks and stones if you do not shut your mouth,' Martello said.

'Go on then,' said Private Dorbell. 'Do what you like, but you didn't ought to talk like that about God. That's blasphemy. Why, you might get struck by lightning for talking that way: you might get all shrivelled up like a bag of crisps. *And* serve you right,' he added, visualising the event with satisfaction.

Martello glared at Dorbell, breathing hard.

'You,' he said at last. 'You I shall shoot personally. And it will take six shots to finish you off. That I guarantee.'

Dorbell said, 'Eee, you're a nasty man. I'll have to pray for you, even if it goes against the grain.'

Martello yelled, 'I change my mind! Now I shoot! You shall be an example!' and lifted his revolver, aimed at Dorbell's heart, and fired.

The force of the bullet spun Dorbell sideways. He fell on hands and knees, coughing almost politely, then rolled round into a squatting position. Ignoring Martello, Widdicombe and Wohlhaber dropped to their knees beside Dorbell.

'Swine,' Widdicombe was muttering. 'Filthy, murdering swine.'

Private Dorbell's hand covered his heart. He rubbed, winced slightly, then stood up.

'I'll be all right, sir,' he said.

Martello's eyes widened, and the partisans fell back, murmuring among themselves, one or two of them crossing themselves atavistically or making signs against the evil eye.

Swiftly Martello said, 'A capitalist trick. Dawn, then.' And to Dorbell: 'Next time I shall make no mistake with you. For you, I use a machine-gun.'

Martello shouted to his companions, who ranged the prisoners in indian file, each man flanked by a partisan and jerked roughly forward to the accompaniment of threats and curses. The rest of the partisans split up into a rear party, a leading group headed by Martello, and scouts on either wing in advance of the main body.

As Major Widdicombe was shoved forward, he gasped at Dorbell, 'Good show! Never thought you could act so convincingly.'

'I don't know what you mean, sir,' said Dorbell.

'I'll talk to you later. My God, you always struck me as a bit of a wet, never saying boo to a goose and so on, but I'll tell you one thing, you're a brave man.'

Major Widdicombe's escort kicked him in the backside and shouted at him to keep moving. Widdicombe rubbed his rear and obeyed, while the partisans began to sing *Bandiera Rossa*, the scouts joining in faintly from the distance and so making themselves superfluous.

Unheard, Private Dorbell said, 'Who, me, brave? And I've had me life saved two separate times in one day. Think of that!'

*   *   *

At twilight they came to a few scruffy hovels on a hill-top, women screaming greetings and children getting underfoot, chickens squawking and fluttering out of the way, dogs barking and chasing the chickens. Martello stood on a rickety farm cart and made a long speech, while nobody paid very much attention, the people of the village busying themselves by fetching bread and wine for every-one, prisoners included. The partisans stopped their general conversation when Martello finished his speech, and they clapped enthusiastically, shouting what Major Widdicombe took to be party parrot-cries.

'That Martello must be the chap who signed the letter to the Countess. Don't say anything to him about the mules,' he warned Trommel and the others, munching the last of his hunk of coarse dark bread and draining his wine. Women were moving among the partisans and prisoners collecting glasses carefully. Widdicombe handed his over to a thin girl with an incipient moustache, then turned away, his stomach suddenly contracted with fear, the palms of his hands growing damp. He thought, The condemned man ate a hearty meal, my God; they're going to shoot us in the morning! Must say old Trommel's taking it calmly. He's got guts. But I'm a coward, I'm afraid to die; I want to live and I want to find those mules.

Major Trommel was watching Widdicombe and think-ing, Look at that man; God, I envy him. British phlegm, solid as a rock, while my fear must be plain for all to see: knees trembling, hands shaking so that I had to use them both to hold my glass; God, I want to live instead of being shot like a dog.

After the women had made their rounds and all the precious glasses had been collected and counted, the parti-sans stored the captured arms in an empty house, then herded the prisoners into a dilapidated hall blazoned with hammers and sickles and scrawled with hortatory slogans. The door was missing, the windows had no glass, but the shutters were fastened and two guards stationed at the doorway. Martello strode into the hall and looked round with grim satisfaction.

'So,' he said. 'This is where you spend your last night on earth. You will sleep on the floor. I regret that we have little in the way of capitalist luxuries here, but the day is coming when we shall have all those things. Every time one of you pigs dies, that day is hastened. Good night, gentlemen.'

As soon as he had gone, Major Trommel said to Widdicombe, 'What a mess we are in, Major!'

Widdicombe nodded gloomily and said to Spud Henryson, 'Now perhaps you believe us—not that it's going to do any good one way or the other.'

Henryson said, 'Sure I believe you now.' He looked at Private Dorbell and said, 'How come you ain't dead? I saw that bullet hit you fair and square, right on the heart.'

He went over to Dorbell and peered at his breast pocket in the gloom.

'There's a bullet-hole,' he said, and shook his head disgustedly. 'Aw, hell, don't tell me: I know. You got a bible in there and it stopped the bullet.'

Dorbell fished in his breast pocket and pulled out a thick, squat volume, pulling the pages apart where they had been impacted together by the bullet, which he located halfway through the book. He rubbed the bullet between finger and thumb.

He said, 'No, not a bible. It's *The Wages of Sin*.'

Corporal White said, 'And to think you wanted to lend it to me. If I'd borrowed that book, Knocker, you'd have been a goner now, a bleeding stiff.'

Sergeant Entwistle took the book and examined it, then

handed it back and said, 'Hamdu l'Illah, mate. You got any more? Enough to go all round? Might come in handy in the morning.'

They relapsed into silence, each preoccupied with his own glum thoughts. After twenty minutes or so Major Trommel was dozing, half aware of a droning voice at some distance. He muttered something to himself, then started into full alertness: Wohlhaber was shaking his arm urgently. It was quite dark in the hall.

'What is it?' he said testily. 'Am I not to be allowed my last night in peace?'

Private Wohlhaber said, 'Listen, sir. It's that Martello. He is making a speech.'

'Martello!' Major Trommel said. 'As far as I can gather, he is always making a speech. Now go to sleep, Wohlhaber.'

Wohlhaber said stubbornly, 'Beg to report, sir, I think the major should come and listen.'

Trommel sighed and got up, following Wohlhaber to a shuttered window. Widdicombe heard them, and came along for the sake of something to do; after a moment Henryson joined them.

'Just listen,' said Wohlhaber to Major Trommel.

They peered through the louvres of the shutter. On the rough space of beaten earth which passed for the hamlet's square a fire had been kindled, and the partisans were sitting round drinking wine and listening to Martello.

'. . . To sum up, then,' he was saying, 'our group will move north on the first of next month. On the second, we come under the direct command of the area commissar. The day before, leading civilian figures will have been executed on various pretexts . . .'

Sismonda, thought Trommel.

'. . . and a full-scale operation of general sabotage against

Allied military installations will have started. But the first of the month will see the beginning of our glorious revolution. We shall seize control of all community centres; Allied town majors, their staffs, and other Allied Military Government personnel will be summarily disposed of. By that time it is confidently predicted that all Allied fighting troops will be many miles to the north, and we shall have only base personnel to deal with.' He slashed a hand of stiff fingers across his throat, and the audience laughed and cheered with enthusiasm. 'Exactly. The province of Emilia is already known as the Red Triangle, because our comrades have gained effective control of local government there. They have done it by more or less peaceful means. We shall do otherwise. Blood will flow, comrades. We shall conquer, and when we have conquered, twenty thousand of us shall march on Rome!'

'*Verflucht nochmal!*' said Major Trommel.

'What's he going on about?' Widdicombe asked.

'I will tell you in a moment. Please keep silent.'

'. . . Our comrades battling heroically in Yugoslavia will join us, the workers in the industrial centres will rise and join us also, and then, comrades, we shall at last be liberated from our so-called liberators!'

Everybody applauded rowdily; Martello sat down and took a large draught of wine; and Major Trommel exhaled a loud sigh.

'Now would you mind telling me what's happening?' said Major Widdicombe.

Should I? thought Major Trommel. Is it not my duty to keep my mouth shut? This may help the Wehrmacht to hold its own, if a huge communist rising should divert the Allies from their relentless northward thrust. Surely I must hold my tongue?

He told Major Widdicombe all he had heard.

'Phew!' said Widdicombe as Major Trommel finished speaking. 'A hornets' nest, that's what we've landed in.'

Spud Henryson said, 'Allied Armies Italy would sure give a lot to know about this.'

'Yes,' Major Widdicombe agreed, 'but it's an academic point. We're going to be shot at dawn. Let's sleep on it.' Then he said sadly, 'It's a funny thing: thought I'd want to stay awake all night, but I feel a bit tired now, and I think I'll have to crash the old swede. Seems a waste of time somehow, going to sleep when you'll be sleeping permanently very soon, if you see what I mean. Still . . .'

He drifted away from the others and lay down on the floor.

Henryson said, 'Gee, those Limeys take some beating. I need a smoke. Got any cigarettes, Major?'

Trommel shook his head, but Wohlhaber pulled out a battered packet of Ardath which Dorbell had given him.

'*Bitte schön*,' he said, handing round cigarettes.

Trommel and Henryson smoked in silence for a while, then they too lay down. Wohlhaber strained his eyes in the darkness, and could just make out the forms of the guards in the doorway. Nine hundred and fifty thousand lire sitting waiting for him in Borgo San Marco, and he was to be shot! He would rest a little while, then rouse the Tommies, and they would try to make a break for it. He nodded to himself sagely, lay down, and immediately fell into a deep sleep.

*   *   *

They were wakened in the chilly half-darkness of early morning, roused up by yells and curses, prods and kicks. Unshaven and thirsty, they stumbled out of the hall and were dragged into line, the officers on the right. Martello sauntered up to them, and to their surprise offered them a tin of Trinciato Nazionale tobacco and a wad of cigarette papers. They declined because none of them knew how to roll cigarettes, and Private Wohlhaber passed round what remained of Dorbell's army issue. Martello looked at Dorbell reflectively.

'I have been thinking about you,' he said. 'You are the type of man we want in our group. Would you care to join us? If so, I shall have pleasure in waiving the death sentence.'

Private Dorbell said, 'I've been praying for you a lot, Mister Martello, and I can see it's done some good. No, I'm not joining up with you, thanks very much all the same.'

Martello sighed, 'As I thought,' and looked at a large silver pocket watch. 'Come then. The will of the people will now be done.'

They were led behind the building to its rear wall, and ranged against it. Six of the partisans formed up some ten yards away, their carbines held loosely, and their eyes fixed on Martello, awaiting the signal to aim.

Martello stood by the firing squad, slightly to one side, and called to the prisoners, 'Do you wish for bandages?'

'What's the use of bandages after we're bleeding well dead?' Corporal White said in a shaky voice.

'No. Bandages for the eyes. You want them?'

Major Trommel said, 'No bandages,' and stubbed out his cigarette with his heel, thinking, That is what the heroes would do.

Henryson said to Martello, 'You wait, you goddam bastard. The United States Army's going to have something to say about this.'

Sergeant Entwistle snarled, 'Ah come on, iggri, get it over with!'

And Major Widdicombe said nothing, leaning back against the wall in a strange peace, thinking, It's funny but I'm proud of them all now, and to think when I first met them I wouldn't have given tuppence ha'penny for the whole boiling of them, myself included if I think back. Pity about Sismonda, though. No more transports of rapture. And I bet some damned great brewery'll buy up the old pub.

He heard Martello shout, 'Aim!' and opened his eyes briefly to see the lifted carbines and in particular the black hole of the muzzle opposite. The others had all instinctively closed their eyes, and he shut his again.

A burst of fire broke out, and a confused shouting. So this is what it feels like, Widdicombe thought. Nothing at all, and I'm dead. I'm dead. Or dying, anyway, and it doesn't even hurt.

The shots continued. Finishing us off, Widdicombe thought as a bullet smacked into the wall by his head. Then he opened his eyes. The firing squad was lying on the ground facing away from the prisoners, and shooting across the unkempt ground behind the hall at some little figures dodging towards them over a slope strewn with boulders. In the faint radiance of the eastern sky Widdicombe saw that the figures wore green scarves.

Wohlhaber clawed at his sleeve, pulling him down into a crouch.

'Quick!' said Major Trommel, and ran for it round the corner of the building, Widdicombe, Wohlhaber and Henryson each treading on the heels of the man in front as they came next, then White and Entwistle.

'Where's Dorbell?' Widdicombe gasped. 'Let's get out of this place.'

They waited, and heard confused shouting through the gunfire, yells of 'Garibaldini!' They heard Martello's voice raised above the others, cracking as he shrieked commands. Dorbell came round the corner at a normal pace.

'Three times,' he said. 'Three times in two days I've had me life saved!'

Major Widdicombe said, 'I shall personally ensure that you lose it unless you hurry up. Come on now, everybody: double out of here.'

Trommel said, 'All the partisans are fighting. Let us find some food on the way. Ha! They will shut in the horse after the stable door has gone.'

They moved stealthily along the side of the hall and turned right. Behind them and to their left the firing continued, and an occasional waspish bullet zipped over their heads until they reached the shelter of a small house. Wohlhaber and Corporal White pushed open the door and went in. There was no one in the tiny front room, but they found a bottle of red wine and a half-eaten loaf.

'Won't go far,' White said, stuffing the bread into his shirt and the bottle into the side pocket of his jacket.

The party went along the line of hovels: more wine, more bread.

'Seems a bit off, taking this stuff,' Major Widdicombe said. 'Might be all they've got.'

Major Trommel said, 'They have sheltered the people who were going to shoot us. We will take it. Bread and wine will keep us going, if not in luxury.'

'And now for God's sake let's high-tail it out of here,' Henryson said.

They moved on, and were passing a small house with a blank door of unpainted wood, when Sergeant Entwistle said to Widdicombe, 'Stan 'esh shwaieh, sir, I mean hang on a minute.' He pointed to the door. 'That's where they put our guns and ammo.'

He tried the door, then stood back, lifting his foot high

and shooting it forward so that the sole of his boot struck the keyhole; the door crashed open.

Five minutes later they were struggling through a tangle of maquis, re-armed and jubilant, giggling with a sort of party spirit, and talking nonstop. As they pushed on, the sound of firing diminished behind them, and after half an hour they halted in a clearing and rested, eating some bread and taking a few swallows of wine.

'Pity we didn't find our rations,' said Major Widdicombe. 'And my air mattress. I shall miss that. And my binoculars.'

'We have our weapons back. And we have bread, wine, and our lives,' Major Trommel said. 'As far as I am concerned, that is sufficient for the moment.'

Widdicombe nodded and said, 'I ought to do something about it.'

'What?'

'That chap Martello. Remember? That plan he was talking about last night. I ought to warn somebody before we do anything else.'

Spud Henryson said, 'It's pretty hot intelligence at that.'

Major Widdicombe looked at him speculatively.

'Do you still think we're cracked?'

'I certainly think you're lucky,' Henryson said. 'Say . . . you really mean what you told me about those mules?'

Widdicombe nodded and said, 'You want to come with us?'

'Hell, no,' said Henryson. 'That's so crazy it's out of this world. I still think there's something else behind it.'

'Certainly,' Major Trommel interjected. 'The life of a lady is at stake. This you know.'

Henryson nodded and was about to reply, but Major

Widdicombe stood up and said, 'You're our man. You ought to go north till you make contact with Allied troops: find a field officer and warn him that the communists are going to take over the whole province on the first of next month. He'll know what to do. How about it?'

'Okay, it's a deal,' Henryson said after some consideration. 'In a way I hate to leave you, but it may make for a quieter life.' He grinned and added, 'I still reckon those mules must be carrying gold or diamonds or sump'n.'

Major Widdicombe shrugged and held out his hand.

'Good luck,' he said.

Henryson shook hands all round, collected what remained of his bread and wine, and moved off. At the edge of the clearing he turned and said, 'One thing has me worried. You said the life of a lady was at stake. You mean *two* of these dames?'

'Two?' said Major Trommel. 'No. One.'

'How come? You're engaged to one, you told me.' Henryson looked at Widdicombe. 'So are you: you said so. And each of these dames is a countess. It doesn't figure.' He shook his head and then said, 'Ah, hell. The whole operation doesn't figure, come to that. I'm going to beat it. So long.'

He waved a hand and was gone. They heard him crashing through the thick scrub until the sound of his passage died away in the distance. Then Major Trommel and Major Widdicombe turned to each other, mouths open and fists raised in rage.

Sergeant Entwistle coughed explosively and said, 'Sir! Major Trommel! Look over here, behind me. Quick!'

Slowly they lowered their fists and looked. Seven figures were standing silently at the opposite end of the clearing to that from which Henryson had left. They wore light-blue scarves and carried small carabiniere-type carbines.

'Gawd!' said Corporal White.

The leading figure stepped forward and said, 'We are the Amazons of the New Italy. And who are you?'

All seven of the newcomers were women.

II

APART from their blue scarves the Amazons of the New Italy wore neat beige blouses, crossed attractively by bandoliers, and navy slacks. They looked at the men impassively, moving forward for a closer inspection as one of them made a signal. Evidently she was the leader: a tall and well-made woman of perhaps thirty-five, with a golden-brown skin and brown hair, the bottoms of her slacks tucked into suède mosquito boots. She looked at them lazily for a while through enigmatic hazel eyes, then smiled, caressing the short muzzle of her carbine.

Major Widdicombe coughed, embarrassed by the length of her scrutiny. He said, 'Er—how do you do?'

The woman turned to him and sauntered closer, looking him up and down.

'Well?' she said. 'Who are you? British and Germans together—are you deserters?'

'Not exactly,' Widdicombe said. 'It's a long story. My name is Widdicombe.' He pointed. 'Major Trommel . . .' and he introduced the rest of the party as though calling the roll on parade, while the woman watched with quiet attention.

'Thank you,' she said. 'I am Tina Menotti. . . . Now: Carla and Carità!'

Two slim girls stepped forward.

'Peas in a pod,' said Sergeant Entwistle in astonishment: the girls were identical twins, blonde and blue-eyed: Carla held her gun in the left hand, and Carità in the right, but that was the only observable difference between them. They smiled and bobbed briefly.

Corporal White said, 'Promising, this is. No one's offered to shoot us yet.'

Tina Menotti called, 'Maria,' and a small, very plump girl with ginger hair smiled and ducked her head coyly.

'Poor lass,' Private Dorbell said. 'She's shy.'

'Luisa.'

Luisa was about forty, with big hands and breasts, long black hair and an olive complexion; she nodded coolly, looking at the men from watchful sloe-eyes: a gaze revealing much expereince of the world, non-committal, relaxed.

'Marta!' said Tina Menotti, and the men looked, swallowed, and looked again. Marta's beauty was electric; feature by feature she was not so pretty as the twins—she had a pale skin, green eyes and smooth black hair, a small, svelte figure—but she also possessed that intangible quality of the kind to make young men walk into walls as they looked after her in the street, and old men come leaping out of wheelchairs.

'Yes,' said Major Widdicombe faintly. 'Marta.'

The girl smiled, and turned to say something to the girl next to her, a plain pudding-face with mouse-brown hair, drab brown eyes and a big mouth.

'That is Dina,' the leader said anticlimatically.

The men grunted off-handedly or said nothing; then Major Trommel spoke.

'Let us get one thing clear,' he said. 'Are you taking us prisoner?'

Tina Menotti said, 'Possibly you and your man. And maybe the others; it all depends. We are against all men, are we not, fellow Amazons?'

'Yes, yes!' they shouted.

'What do men do?'

'They enslave women,' came the chorus. 'They beat us, lie to us, cheat us of our rights.'

'And what is the aim of the Amazons of the New Italy?'

'To fight till we have our rights.'

'You see,' said Tina Menotti. 'We are determined to have our rights. We are a small movement, but we shall grow, and the female sex shall conquer!'

Major Widdicombe said gallantly, 'My dear lady, let me assure you that it has conquered me already,' and Major Trommel gave a disappointed nod of agreement: disappointed because he had been about to say exactly the same thing.

Instead he said, 'Equality for women, and all that sort of thing?'

'Equality!' the woman snorted. 'Not equality. Superiority. In our world the women will give the orders.'

Trommel shrugged and said, 'Spare us the speeches, please; we have had rather too many of late. And what are your orders now?'

Tina Menotti said, 'We are in the territory of the Garibaldini.'

'Garibaldini?' Major Widdicombe frowned. 'Heard that name before. Let's see, it was when we got away from that chap Martello.'

'Martello is a communist,' the woman said in surprise.

'Quite. And he was going to shoot us. Then these chaps in green scarves attacked his camp, and we got away. People were shouting about Garibaldini.'

'Ah,' she said. 'The ones in the green scarves, they are Garibaldini. They are many and we are few. They hunt us constantly.'

'Good heavens,' Widdicombe said. 'Whatever for?' Then he looked round at the women and added, 'Oh yes, I see what you mean. Poor show.'

'You have automatic weapons and grenades. If we meet the Garibaldini you can give us supporting fire.'

'That will be a pleasure,' Major Trommel said. 'We are travelling in a generally southerly direction, and we shall be glad to help so long as you do not take us too far out of our way. We are searching for a mule train . . .'

Trommel gave a brief account of their objective and of their progress so far; and when he had finished, Tina Menotti deliberated carefully before speaking.

At length she said, 'I think we should join forces for a time. By yourselves you would stand no more chance of getting through the Garibaldini than we, but together, yes. However, you must place yourselves under our command. In the new world, women shall give the orders.'

'Right you are,' Major Widdicombe said, while Trommel looked at him with scorn.

'Impossible. A major of the Wehrmacht does not take orders from women,' he said. 'Your new world has not come about yet, and it is no use pricking against the kicks by pretending that it has.'

Widdicombe said, 'Look, why argue? Let's just all go along together.'

'I must command.' Tina was adamant. 'After all, I know the country and you do not.'

'Oh, all right,' said Widdicombe. 'Who the hell cares, anyhow? Look, Trommel old sausage, let her lead. Just till we get through these chaps in the green scarves, and then we'll be saying goodbye to these ladies. Just this once?'

Major Trommel said, 'Under protest, mark you. Under protest.'

*   *   *

The order of march settled down quickly, with Tina leading, then Trommel. Luisa's tall figure came next, topping Trommel by a head; she strode along easily with Widdicombe behind her. The twins, Carla and Carità, walked in front of Sergeant Entwistle, then came Maria. Wohlhaber preceded Dina, who was followed by Corporal White, then Marta, and finally Dorbell brought up the rear, plodding along and averting his gaze from the enchanting hindquarters of the New Amazons' loveliest member. A most unmilitary whiff of perfume reached his nostrils, elusive and tantalising.

'Phoo!' said Dorbell to himself aloud, sniffing fearfully. 'Mebbe I ought to have joined up with that Marteller after all.'

Marta glanced over her shoulder as he spoke; her eyebrows raised quizzically, smiling as she looked; Dorbell flushed and glared at his boots in confusion. Marta shrugged and walked on. Ten minutes later, Tina at the head of the column held up her hand suddenly, and all halted except Private Dorbell, who carried on as usual. This time, however, he was brought up short by Marta and not Corporal White. They reeled together, Dorbell putting out his hands to save himself and falling forward against Marta's side, one of his hands encountering a protuberance of disturbingly and paradoxically firm softness beneath the blouse. She pulled away gently, patting at her hair as hisses for silence passed down the line. Dorbell thought, You clumsy clod, doing that to a nice innocent little thing like her, even if it was by accident.

Up at the front of the column Tina was standing frozen, one hand outstretched as she pointed down a little defile to a clearing in the scrubby undergrowth.

'Garibaldini!' she whispered, shrinking against Major Widdicombe, her eyes wide as though in fear. He put an arm round her, enjoying the contact, and saw perhaps thirty green-scarved men squatting round a dying fire, chewing meat and drinking wine, their weapons at their sides.

'They will catch us and ravish us all,' Tina hissed.

Widdicombe opened his mouth in astonishment; the woman pulled away from him and said, 'Fool, I mean all the women. Get down or they will see us.'

She made urgent gestures to the others, and they all crouched obediently, making various cracklings and rustlings.

'We shall have to creep through,' she said, her mouth quivering. 'Oh, we shall be caught. I know we shall be caught and all my little chickens will be dishonoured by those beasts, one after the other! What shall we do?'

'Search me,' Widdicombe said.

Tina grasped his arm and said bravely, 'Luisa and I will sacrifice ourselves. We will creep some distance and then draw their attention. We are the oldest. They will leap upon us, and then you can escape with my little humming-birds.'

Luisa nodded and said darkly, 'About fifteen men each. I am ready.'

'Do not be silly,' Major Trommel said. 'I have a much better idea. Pass the word for Wohlhaber and that big sergeant.'

Entwistle and Wohlhaber wriggled their way to the head of the line, and Trommel said, 'Wohlhaber, give the sergeant three grenades and remind me to note their expenditure on the ammunition-state report when we get back.' Wohlhaber obeyed. 'Now then, Sergeant, you will throw the grenades as far as you can over there'—he pointed to the opposite end of the clearing—'and take out each pin immediately before you throw. Ready? *Now!*'

An enormously fat member of the Garibaldini had produced a piano-accordion and was playing '*Ma l'amore no*' as the first grenade sailed overhead and into the brushwood; then another, and another, the first exploding as the third landed, and the accordion died with a wheezing groan. The next two grenades went off one after the other, and then the Garibaldini were lying on the ground yelling and cursing, the fat man's head beneath the accordion's extended folds. Someone was shouting orders, then they were all firing madly into the undergrowth. In the chatter and rattle of the firing there was no need for silence, and as Tina held up her arm and beckoned, the whole column crashed away out of sight and into safety.

'Fifteen men,' said Luisa flatly when they stopped to regain their breath.

'Yes, dear,' Tina said. 'It would have been too much of a sacrifice.'

'Oh, I don't know; I survived a squadron of Marocchini south of Rome in nineteen-forty-three. I often think back to that day,' she said with a touch of wistfulness.

'Remember your ideals,' Tina told her sharply.

'Yes,' she said with a sigh. 'Yes, I was forgetting.'

Widdicombe was busy congratulating Major Trommel on his stratagem while this conversation was taking place, so Trommel did not hear it. He turned to the women and said, 'Ha, well, you have escaped. My little ruse worked, eh?'

'So would ours have done,' Luisa said ungratefully.

*　　　　*　　　　*

They moved on until the late afternoon, still treading the endless path through the maquis, and met no more people that day. Major Widdicombe no longer felt inconvenienced by his flat feet, and indeed was experiencing a feeling of robust well-being; he thought, Good God I haven't felt like this since those jolly old days in the Boy Scouts, shoving the trek-cart along, it's grand to feel fit and ready for anything. Anything? By gosh, that Tina has a fine stern, not that she can compare with the little piece, what's her name? Marta. Coarr. Now hold on, remember Sismonda. And that reminds me I've got a bone to pick with bloody old Trommel. Dinosaur size. . . .

And Major Trommel walked, breathing easily and as deeply as his chest permitted, thinking, This is *fabelhaft*, I haven't felt like this since I was a little Wanderbird toddling through the Black Forest singing innocent songs and sharpening my dagger with 'Blood and Honour' engraved on its blade. Some blood, some honour. But it was good to walk through the trees on the pine needles, and it is good now; better, in fact. Major Widdicombe showed me the error of my ways: perhaps for me this is the path by which I shall find honour, self-respect, and all those virtues which I thought I had but never came within whistling distance of. . . . This Luisa is a fine upstanding woman, not to be compared with that little piece Marta, and a trifle swarthy for my taste, but still. . . . Now hold on, remember Sismonda. Sismonda? Widdicombe? That reminds me of what the American said. Talk to Widdicombe later. . . .

In the slanting light of early evening they reached a spinney of small trees and a rabbit-shaven greensward sloping gently before the spinney to a little stream flowing from a spring. In the trees they saw a white hut with logs and brushwood stacked against one side.

'Our headquarters,' Tina said proudly. 'Tonight you shall be our guests.'

The men sat down and rested, watching as Carla and Carità took kindling inside the hut; plump, shy Maria disappeared after them with plain Dina; smoke began to rise from the chimney; and very soon, appetising smells of cooking came from the hut, making the men fidget and salivate.

Sergeant Entwistle said to Corporal White, 'What price the field kitchen now, Blacky? If I touch me belly I can feel me backbone through the skin.'

Corporal White grunted and said, 'Food's about all we'll get. Did you hear what they were going on about? They don't seem to want to have nothing to do with men.'

'Right and proper, that is,' said Private Dorbell; and Marta smiled at him from where she sat on the grass cleaning her carbine.

'Ah, peace and quiet!' Major Widdicombe said, looking round. 'Marvellous place, this.' And then he asked Tina Menotti, 'How long have you been here?'

'Five months,' she told him. 'It is five months since my decision. I informed my pig of a husband that I was going to make a new life and fight for a new Italy. He slapped me, so I hit him over the head with a china rolling-pin, shook off my shackles, and took to the woods. Pah! All these other groups of partisans, they are fighting for causes which soon will be dead. The war will finish, and then what? Nothing. But our struggle will continue.'

'Goodness,' Major Widdicombe said, impressed. 'Five months is a long time. I mean, you must miss your husband and—er, and so forth.'

'Nonsense,' she said abruptly.

Major Trommel had sat down on the grass and had closed his eyes, savouring the cooking scents. Something soft and heavy descended, and he opened his eyes to find Luisa stretched out with her head in his lap. He gazed down in astonishment, then tentatively put out a hand and stroked her hair; she gave a purr.

'Luisa!'

At Tina's shout, Luisa shot upright, smoothing down her slacks and looking sheepish.

'I'm sorry,' she said apologetically. 'I—I dozed off.'

Tina tossed her head and turned back to Major Widdicombe, talking formally and earnestly about the rights of women, while Major Trommel stood up and said to Luisa, 'Please don't apologise. I assure you there is nothing to be sorry about.'

Luisa said, 'No. No. You are right, of course,' in a slow, melancholic way, then rushed suddenly inside the hut. From her seat between White and Wohlhaber, Marta watched Luisa go, and smiled still at Private Dorbell.

They dined on rabbit and pasta, finished the bread and wine, and then drank more wine from a demijohn which Maria brought from the hut. The shadows lengthened and the light began to fade from the sky. Wohlhaber and Dorbell made a large fire outside the hut, and they all sat round it conversing in words or signs until it was quite dark, and the leaping flames and occasional showers of sparks were the only light; a thin high covering of cloud hid the stars. Luisa had stayed inside the hut. Carla collected plates with her left hand, while Carità collected them with her right, and plain Dina suddenly began to sing in a high, pure soprano, a song which none of the men knew but which had a melody as plaintive as the calling of curlews on the far northern shores which they had known only too well. The fire died eventually; the men took armfuls of brushwood and made sleeping places for themselves apart under the trees, sighed, yawned, and slept. For a while.

*   *   *

Major Widdicombe opened his eyes and reached for his gun in the same instant, then dropped the gun and peered up in the darkness as he smelt a woman's scent. It was Tina.

'Ssh,' she said, and then murmured, 'It seemed a pity we could not continue our discussion at leisure.'

'Um?' said Widdicombe, blinking himself properly awake. 'Oh, of course. Carry on talking, you mean.'

'Talk enters into it,' Tina said, dropping down beside him with a creak and a rustle of springy twigs. 'Assuredly, there has to be talk.'

'The rights of women, and all that?'

'Indubitably,' she said softly, pulling the lobe of his ear. 'The first rule is that the women give the orders. And I feel . . . very commanding.'

*   *   *

Private Wohlhaber awoke in a wood full of murmurings, sensing a presence near him. He rolled sideways on his couch of brushwood, the Schmeisser in his hands, and then saw the glimmer of a girl's face above him. He dropped the Schmeisser and grabbed the girl's hair, pulling her down and recognising the homely features of Dina. She giggled and bit him fiercely on the nose, then sat on his stomach and tickled his ribs.

She said, 'I am a beach ball: come and bounce me.'

'That is immodest,' Wohlhaber said.

'But I leave modesty to the pretty ones. And even the pretty ones take it off at night with their stockings.'

*   *   *

Major Trommel groaned and stirred. Someone was tugging his arm. He opened his eyes and sat up.

'Is that you, Wohlhaber?' he said. 'What the devil do you want?'

'It is Luisa,' a voice said quietly. 'Get up and come with me. I have something in the hut which I should like to show you.'

Trommel rose and found his hand clasped by Luisa's; she led him through the trees, which were filled with rustlings and strange whisperings: Funny, he thought, There's no breeze. And then they were inside the hut in darkness which was quite impenetrable.

'What is it?' he asked. 'What do you want to show me?'

A pause, a gentle susurrus.

'This.'

Trommel gulped and said to himself, Sismonda, forgive me.

       *   *   *

Sergeant Entwistle awoke with his head on something full and soft: firm warm skin, which struck him as odd because he had fallen asleep on a pillow composed of his pullover wrapped round his boots. He investigated, and found that his head had been resting on shy Maria's bosom. Her head was turned away from him, and her eyes were closed, he discovered; her breath was coming quickly through parted lips.

Sergeant Entwistle shaped his mouth in a soundless whistle, considered for a moment, and made certain dispositions. And then:

'Are you asleep?' he asked.

Maria nodded her head, still keeping it averted.

'I thought you were shy,' said the sergeant, breathing heavily and pursuing his researches.

'Oh yes,' said a little voice. 'Very shy. But I dream a lot. It is surprising what I dream of. Shall I tell you what I am dreaming of now?'

'Don't bother; ma'aleesh,' said Sergeant Entwistle. 'Let me tell you.'

*   *   *

Private Dorbell sat up thinking, The Germans I mean the communists I mean gracious goodness me, well I never did!

He swallowed down his panic as he descried the faint pale oval of Marta's face hovering disembodied above him, smiling, an ethereal version of the Cheshire Cat.

'What you doing here?' he demanded.

The face approached inexorably.

'I say,' Dorbell said anxiously, 'don't you think you ought to be in bed?'

The face nodded, coming still closer, warm breath on Dorbell's cheek making him shrink like a salted snail.

Dorbell said, 'Hop it, this isn't right at all. You mustn't. . . . Hey, go away!'

He clutched *The Wages of Sin* as the face met his, and he could retreat no longer, his back pressed against the bole of a tree. Cool lips touched his, becoming hotter, hotter, and he was spinning in a vortex of uncharted sensation, two slim warm arms wound round his neck, *The Wages of Sin* dangling from his limp fingers. The arms detached themselves, the face moved away, the sensations faded, and a shadow began to recede.

Private Dorbell said, 'Hey, come here!'

The shadow paused, turned, held out its arms. Dorbell ran forward, and with a teasing laugh the shadow ran off through the trees. Dorbell growled, kicked his book so hard that it flew into the sky with pages twittering, then he ran through the trees in pursuit of the shadow, a race of maenad and satyr under the starless sky, Dorbell of the horned brow leaping on cloven feet till the race was won.

*   *   *

And in another part of the wood Corporal White awoke with no especial surprise to see a blonde twin gazing down at him and smiling. He thought, It's a good life, take it by and large, and reached up, pulling the girl gently down.

'Which one are you?' he asked, and she caressed his cheek with her left hand. 'Oh yes, I know now.'

And the night passed in the wood full of noises, and all of them knew they were really dreaming and not doing whatever they appeared to be doing; and more particularly Corporal White, for after sleep and waking, and more sleep he awoke and said to the figure at his side, 'Pity about that twin of yours if she's the odd girl out on this little picnic.'

The girl beside him shook her head, understanding nothing of what he said as she caressed his cheek with her right hand.

12

THEY trudged in silence, each absorbed in his own thoughts and memories, while behind them the morning shadows of the hills shortened as the sun rose higher. Now and again one of them would glance back, hoping even at that distance to catch a glimpse of light blue against the prevailing browns and dull greens and purples of the landscape; but there was nothing. They carried fresh bread and wine, hard cheese and little pebbly onions to sustain them, together with their individual recollections of the night. Before them the path wound downward and then soared round the shoulder of a great bare hill. Major Widdicombe regarded it with distaste.

He said, 'We'll never find those bloody mules.'

'I know,' said Major Trommel with a sigh of fatigue and regret. 'It is hopeless.'

'They wanted us to stay,' Widdicombe said gloomily.

Major Trommel said, 'We could have stopped for a couple of days, perhaps.'

'No, what I mean is this: their camp is on the path, near as dammit. If those mules are coming up the path, then they'd have to pass the camp, wouldn't they? Stands to reason.'

'You mean we could go back and wait there until the mules come past?'

'That's right,' Major Widdicombe said.

They both slowed their pace and looked at each other. Major Trommel said, 'We could turn back now. It is a great temptation.'

'I know,' said Major Widdicombe.

They stopped and let the others plod past them; Major Trommel rubbed his chin and said dreamily, 'Just to sit there and let the mules come to us, while—hrr'm, we rested.'

'And so on,' Widdicombe said.

'Precisely.'

Widdicombe looked back, biting his lip. Then he said, 'No. We can't do it. Not really.'

'Why not?' demanded Major Trommel.

'Sismonda,' said Widdicombe simply. 'If we sit and wait for the mules to come to us instead of getting after them as fast as we can, it may be too late.'

Trommel frowned.

'I am surprised that you can find time to think of her,' he said sarcastically. 'Especially after last night.'

Widdicombe said, 'The same goes for you. I vote we bar all mention of last night. It's done nobody any harm, and it's done Dorbell a power of good: he was skipping along like a spring lamb earlier on.'

They moved along, hurrying to catch the others, and Major Trommel said, 'There is one more thing. I am bound to say, Major, that I have been cherishing a snake in the grass in my bosom. I remind myself of what the American said. What have you been doing with my Sismonda?'

'*Your* Sismonda?' Widdicombe halted again. 'What the hell do you mean?'

'We have been lovers for a long time,' Major Trommel said. 'I have always understood that I should marry her after the war is over.'

'I don't believe you,' Widdicombe said, aghast. 'Anyway, even if there's an atom of truth in what you're saying, it's all finished. You have been discarded, Trommel, cast off like an old glove. Sismonda is mine.'

They glared at each other.

'What do you think we were doing when Sismonda and I left you, and she convinced me to come with you after the mules?' Major Trommel said unpleasantly. 'We were not playing backgammon; oh no: front gammon is more the ticket, I think.'

Major Widdicombe struck himself on both temples with his fists and cried, 'Oh, you dirty dog! Oh, the frightful cow! And to think I'd been in bed with her not twelve hours before!'

Major Trommel blenched and said, 'You are a hateful swinehound, *Schwein und Oberschwein!* Ach, and she is a deceiving temptress, an idol with legs of straw. I have a good mind to give myself up at once to the authorities.'

'I've a good mind to go straight back to the Amazons,' said Widdicombe, more practically. 'Just as long as you're not there, you stinker.'

Again they moved off, Major Trommel walking with his chin high and his eyes frosty, Widdicombe gazing morosely at the ground. They did not speak again until they had left behind them the dip in the path and were breasting the rise; the others were out of sight round the shoulder of the hill. After a few minutes Widdicombe glanced at Major Trommel, and saw to his astonishment that Trommel was weeping silently, the tears streaming down his face and disappearing down the crevice between his collar and his stringy neck. Widdicombe became embarrassed.

He coughed and said, 'I say, look here, you shouldn't take it like that. Be a man, hey?'

'You have stolen everything away from me,' Major Trommel said in a cracked voice. 'First you have stolen away my beliefs, and now you have taken my loved one away from me. There is nothing left. What is the use now to struggle onward, *immer hinaufzustreben* for a miserable herd of mules?'

Major Widdicombe said, 'Don't be silly. Those mules are damned important—to Sismonda, to Borgo San Marco, and to us. Never mind who's going to get Sismonda. Matter of fact, I believe she must be testing us.'

'Testing us? That she has already done,' Trommel said bitterly.

'No, I mean over those mules. If we come back with them, then she'll choose: see what I'm getting at? Like those damsels did with knights of old and so on.'

'She is an aristocrat,' Trommel said thoughtfully, nodding; he blew his nose and wiped his face, growing more cheerful.

'Right. Now leave that for a minute. We're in a hell of a fix: neither of us dares go back to his own troops. Is that correct?' Trommel nodded, and Major Widdicombe went on, 'Now then, if we find those mules and take 'em back to the village, why, we'll be the heroes of the hour. We'll be able to hole up there till the fighting's over, then wait a few months and everything in the garden'll be lovely. If Sismonda chooses me, you'll be able to stay with us till you can sneak back to Germany; if she chooses you, then I'll blossom out as a tourist when things have settled down.'

Major Trommel said, puffing a little as the slope increased, 'A hero. Heroes. You really think so?'

'Absolutely.'

'I have always wanted to be a hero,' Trommel said wistfully.

'I've always wanted to *do* something, too, and this is the

only chance we're likely to get. I don't think we ought to spoil it by quarrelling over a woman.'

Trommel said, 'Major, I am very sorry if I was angry with you. You are capable of inspirations, and I must make allowance for that.'

'No hard feelings?'

'None at all,' said Major Trommel, and they shook hands gravely.

*　　　*　　　*

As they rounded the shoulder of the hill, Widdicombe and Trommel saw the others lying on the ground peering through the brushwood, with the exception of Sergeant Entwistle, who crouched facing the officers and making furious gestures to them to keep low. Bent double, they joined him, and he pointed downward.

'Look there, sir,' he said to Widdicombe, who gazed to where the path wound down before rising to the next hill.

He saw the mules. There seemed to be a lot of them, standing quietly strung out along the track, each carrying a pair of barrels. Men on foot stood by them, surrounded by a number of others on horseback holding rifles and menacing them.

'The mules!' said Widdicombe. 'But what's happening?'

Major Trommel said, 'Those men on horses are brigands. What did I tell you?'

At the head of the mule train stood a swarthy figure with a gaudy spotted handkerchief knotted over his head, and an equally garish scarf round his neck; large gold or brass rings glinted at his ears. Like all the standing men, four of them, his hands were raised, and he was staring defiantly at the leader of the half-dozen mounted men, a huge and bloated shape with its back to the watchers.

Widdicombe said, 'We'll have to do something about this. Sergeant, pass the word along. When I fire, everybody jump up and run down the hill shooting for all you're worth.'

'Sir,' said Entwistle, and crawled forward to the others, while Trommel whispered the order to Wohlhaber.

Better fire a shot over their heads, Widdicombe thought. As he drew his gun, the leader of the brigands turned slightly, showing a fat red face: he reached over to the nearest mule and rummaged in a saddle-bag by the barrel, coming up with a bottle of wine. He slung his rifle and un-corked the bottle, tilting back his head and drinking deeply. Major Widdicombe aimed at an imaginary point twenty feet above the man's nose, fired, and was astonished to see the bottle disintegrate in the man's hand, splashing him with red wine and showering fragments around. At once all the others leaped up, running down the hill and firing at ran-dom; Major Widdicombe recovered himself, blew the smoke nonchalantly from the muzzle of his pistol and followed. The brigands were yelling, their horses' hoofs drumming wildly as they scattered. In a few moments they had vanished into the maquis.

'See,' Trommel said as Major Widdicombe joined him, 'we have put them to flight. A magnificent shot, Major: please allow me to congratulate you.'

'It was nothing.' Widdicombe shrugged modestly.

The muleteers were busy calming their mules, which were bucking and snorting, but eventually the leader came over to the rescuers, grabbed Major Widdicombe by the hand and shook it up and down, speaking volubly.

'What's he say?' Widdicombe asked.

Major Trommel shook his head and said, 'I have no idea. He is not speaking Italian.' He turned to the man and said, '*Italiano?*'

'*Romani. Zingaro,*' said the man.

'Perhaps he is a Roumanian,' Trommel said doubtfully.

'I dunno . . .' Widdicombe appraised the man and his companions and then said, 'Looks a sort of a diddicoy to me. Like Hitler, only this one's moustache is a sight bigger, and so's his nose. But he could be a diddicoy.'

The man drew himself up, eyes flashing, and spat on the ground.

'*Diddikai,*' he said with infinite contempt, shaking his head. '*Romani!*'

'Oh, I've got it,' Widdicombe said. 'Romany. He's a gipsy.'

The man pointed to himself and said, 'Nasellino,' and then gestured at Major Widdicombe's revolver, said, 'Bam!' and chuckled delightedly.

Widdicombe sat down at the side of the track, suddenly weary, overcome by a sense of anticlimax.

'Well, we've done it,' he said to Trommel. 'We've found the mules. All we have to do now is get 'em back to Borgo San Marco. God, I could do with a drink: a good stiff tot of something with a kick like one of those creatures there.'

Trommel said, 'Major Widdicombe, some day when all this is over, you shall come to Germany and I will entertain you, and we shall look back to this moment as the finest in our lives. Do not feel disappointed that we have achieved our objective: be proud.'

Widdicombe sighed and said, 'I know, but somehow for me the journey is more important than the journey's end.'

'It is a long way back to Borgo San Marco,' said Trommel. 'If those brigands should come after us, the journey may be far from having ended.'

Major Widdicombe perked up and said, 'You're right. I never thought of it that way.'

He got to his feet and wandered along the path looking at the mules, twelve of them, haltered and roped together, each carrying its pair of barrels. Entwistle and White were shouting and making signs to the other muleteers, offering cigarettes, while the muleteers were laughing, clapping shoulders and shaking hands. At the side of the path Dorbell and Wohlhaber were making a fire.

'Jolly good,' Major Widdicombe said. 'Tea up soon, hey? Pity we haven't got any milk.'

He went back to Nasellino and tapped his arm, then said, 'Milk? Got any milk?' grasping imaginary teats and pumping vigorously, then pretending to drink. The gipsy nodded and called to one of the muleteers, who ferreted in a sack tied in front of a barrel and came over with a small can of evaporated milk, U.S. Army issue. He gave it to Nasellino, who presented it to Major Widdicombe with a flourish.

'Well, thanks very much,' Widdicombe said.

The British drank tea, while Trommel and Wohlhaber drank coarse red wine, and all shared a meal of dark bread, olives and salami with the gipsies. They kept a careful watch for the brigands when at length the party moved off, but saw no one.

'They won't come back,' Corporal White said.

Entwistle said, 'Some bloody hopes after that shot of our bloke's. That beat the Kittyhawk, that did.'

*   *   *

Private Dorbell moistened his lips as the mule train neared the New Amazons' camp, guilt and expectancy engaged on a heavyweight wrestling match in his soul.

He said to Wohlhaber, 'Rooning through the woods after a lass. It was all a dream.'

Wohlhaber nodded uncomprehendingly.

'No, it wonna,' Dorbell said sternly. 'Telling lies won't help. I was keeping meself pure for Aggie Bircumshaw, and now look what! I can see her face now, singing "Rock of Airges", and me giving out with me chooba. If they find out, I'll get droomed out of the Army.'

Private Wohlhaber grunted.

'I ought to feel condemned,' Dorbell said. 'I've been trying and trying all day to feel condemned, and all I can think of is this. That there Aggie Bircumshaw's a doompy little cow. I'd rather stop in Italy and grow macaroni.'

And Major Widdicombe said to Major Trommel, 'Look, there's the hut now. Can't see anyone about. Perhaps they're all out fighting the Garibaldini or something. Tell you what: we'll halt the mules here, and if the girls are in we'll tell old Vaselino or whatever he's called to hang on for half an hour while we—er'm, say goodbye, what?'

'A short farewell walk in the woods,' Major Trommel agreed gravely.

After making it clear to the muleteers that they were to remain, the party walked up to the hut avoiding one another's eyes, stepping carefully as though the sward were strewn with obstacles, until at last they reached the door.

'I can hear noises,' Wohlhaber said to Major Trommel, and Sergeant Entwistle said, 'Listen: someone laughing.'

'Yes,' said Major Widdicombe, shaken. 'In a man's voice.'

They all stared at one another. Wohlhaber tiptoed to the little window and peered through a crack in the shutters; the others joined him and elbowed him out of the way one by one.

'Oh, my God,' said Major Widdicombe.

13

PRIVATE DORBELL was the last to apply his eye to the crack in the shutter; ignoring the forms of the other girls and men as they lay sprawled round the floor of the hut or sat at the kitchen table, he saw only Marta leaning back in the arms of a tall, ginger-haired young man in denim overalls who was kissing her deeply and at the same time removing her blouse. She snuggled closer, saying something in a warm and murmurous voice, and the man laughed for a second time. Dorbell stood away from the crack and began to cry quietly.

Major Trommel shrugged and said to Widdicombe, 'The rights of women are getting plenty of exercise. But who are the men?'

Widdicombe shook his head, but Sergeant Entwistle said, 'I know what they are, sir. They're American para-troopers. They must have dropped somewhere nearby.'

'And landed on their feet,' Corporal White said acidly.

Trommel and Widdicombe stared at each other in horror.

'Americans?' Trommel said, looking suddenly collapsed.

Widdicombe thought, Bloody hell, he looks about ninety-seven, and ten minutes ago I was thinking how this trip was doing wonders for him.

He said, 'Quick. Everybody back to the mules. We're getting out of here like the clappers.'

Major Trommel said slowly, 'Then you are not going to turn me over to the Americans?'

Impatiently Widdicombe said, 'Have some sense. They've got much more interesting things to think about. If we interrupted them now, they'd shoot us all out of hand. Come on. Sergeant, you and Corporal White see to Dorbell.'

They hurried back to the mules, Dorbell allowing himself to be led sniffing and hiccuping away, and Trommel impressed upon Nasellino the need for silence in starting the mule train moving. Nasellino nodded, the big ear-rings flashing and dancing. He understood standard Italian, but spoke only Romany and an incomprehensible southern dialect. Then he spoke to his muleteers, who urged the mules forward with whispers, instead of the usual barrage of curses and whipcracks. Not one of them moved.

Widdicombe groaned, 'For God's sake hurry up.'

The leading mule's name was Ciurcill. It stood patiently but immobile, taking its weight on three legs.

'Ciurcill!' hissed Nasellino.

Ciurcill cocked an eye at its master, then looked back at the ground.

'Ciurcill! *Avant*, *fangusc'!*' Nasellino said.

The mule shifted its weight to all four hoofs, rooting itself to the earth. Nasellino took out a box of matches, extracted half a dozen which he held together, striking them all at once and applying the flaming torch to the tip of Ciurcill's tail. The mule roared, laid back its ears and lashed out with its hind legs, the hoofs scything the air inches from Nasellino's head; and then it was jerking the other mules down the path at a smart trot. Trommel was in agony lest the noise should bring the Americans out of the hut to investigate, but Major Widdicombe's assessment proved correct.

Safely round a bend in the path, Sergeant Entwistle said, 'Just the bloody same at home. Take a bint to the pictures, nip out of your seat for two minutes to have a jimmy-riddle, and you come back to find she's necking with a Yank.'

Corporal White said, 'Not to worry. They're all the same, women are. The only way to keep 'em safe is to put 'em in tin knickers.'

'And every G.I. carries a can-opener,' Entwistle said gloomily. Then he brightened. 'Oh well, it's not as if we was going to marry 'em.'

'*I* was,' said a small voice. 'And now I've been and gone and broke me heart.'

And further up the line Major Trommel said to Major Widdicombe, 'Thank you.' He drew his pistol and held it out butt foremost to Widdicombe.

'If this area is under Allied control,' he said, 'then Wohlhaber and I are now your prisoners again. Please. I count it an honour.'

'Well, if you insist,' said Widdicombe, touched. 'But I wouldn't dream of taking your gun. We've been through too much together.'

Trommel wiped away a tear and blew his nose.

'You are too chivalrous,' he said. 'For you I will renounce my claim to Sismonda's hand.'

'Jolly decent offer, that,' said Widdicombe, over-whelmed. 'But we'll have to let her choose. When the war's over you must come and stay with me at my pub.'

'Thank you. But if you marry Sismonda you will stay in Italy, surely?'

Major Widdicombe said, 'No. I've been thinking it over. I'm not really cut out for that sort of life. And another thing: Sismonda would look absolutely marvellous behind the bar.'

*   *   *

They made a long march that day, and camped at last when the stars were out, sharing the muleteers' food as before. They sat round the dying fire and listened as one of the gipsies played a harmonica and Nasellino sang in a rough bass voice, while in the background Private Dorbell sat with his head on his knees, Wohlhaber by his side in mute sympathy. They all slept deeply, and woke to a day of uneventful plodding along the track, the muleteers making routine noises at their beasts more to relieve the boredom of the journey than for any other reason. Both Widdicombe and Trommel were concerned as they passed through the Garibaldini territory into that of the communists, but they met no one at all: the world had narrowed to a string of mules. Ciurcill gave no more trouble, biding its time until Nasellino should forget himself and come within range of its rear hoofs, a forlorn hope. At several places Nasellino turned the mule train off the path to water the existence of which Widdicombe and Trommel had never suspected on their outward journey. Again dusk fell, and again they slept.

The following morning they moved off at first light. After a couple of hours they came to a fork in the path. The left branch led straight on, while the right doubled back on itself and took a generally south-easterly direction. Nasellino was leading the mule train on to the right-hand path when Major Widdicombe shouted at him to halt.

'That's the wrong way,' he said, gesticulating at the left-hand fork. 'There. That's the way to Borgo San Marco.'

Nasellino shook his head and said something which sounded like 'Shezhoin.'

Trommel said, 'I do not know what he means, but you are right, Major. The way is straight on,' and he spoke to the gipsy in Italian. Again Nasellino shook his head, pointing with finality down the right-hand fork; the other muleteers muttered in evident agreement.

'Damn it all,' said Widdicombe, 'the fellow's as stubborn as his own blasted mules.'

Major Trommel yelled at Nasellino, 'Left, left!'

Nasellino scowled and spat at Major Trommel's feet, saying something angrily in his atrocious dialect.

'I bet he wants to take the oil and flog it somewhere,' Major Widdicombe said in horror. 'Sergeant!'

'Sir?' said Entwistle.

'These mules are going to Borgo San Marco. If necessary, they're going at gunpoint. Now keep these men covered, you and Corporal White.'

'Yessir.'

Entwistle and White raised their guns; the muleteers stood frozen, Nasellino's expression darkened with hatred.

'Now turn left,' Trommel said to him in Italian.

Nasellino turned his back on Major Trommel, wiped his hand on the seat of his trousers with contempt, and then called disgustedly to his muleteers. They took the left fork.

*   *   *

Gradually the vegetation became sparser, the stark rock out-cropping from the poor soil, and at four o'clock in the afternoon they halted on the twisting path, high above Borgo San Marco and to the westward. Near the path was a flat rock; Major Trommel glanced at it and said to Widdicombe, 'Here is where the sergeant knocked me out. It all seems so long ago.'

Widdicombe did not reply: he was scanning the village below for signs of military activity. There was none, and he turned to Trommel happily.

'Well, here we are,' he said. 'Here we are at last! By golly, I can't wait to see Sismonda's face when we show her the mules. She'll have something pretty sharp to say to this gipsy bod as well, I shouldn't wonder.'

He waved his pistol at Nasellino, who grunted sourly and motioned the muleteers on, grumbling viciously to himself. The mules began to climb down the twisting track, slowly but with a casual sureness of foot. Major Widdicombe's sensation of anticlimax had passed as soon as the quarrel with Nasellino had begun, and now he was excited and elated, thinking, By God, we've done it! Here we come with the mules, we'll be the heroes of Borgo San Marco if we can't be heroes any other way; feel as though I'd just won a battle or something; can't wait to see Sismonda's face, and then hey-ho from transport of mules to transports of rapture.

They reached the outskirts of the village. A small boy whom Private Dorbell remembered was playing trains, shuffling his feet and chuffing to himself, still announcing imminent departure for Naples; but at sight of the mule train he stopped, gaped, and then ran ahead yelling. In a few moments the party were struggling through a small crowd of cheering, laughing villagers. A brass band materialised in hastily donned, tattered blue uniforms with silver epaulettes—cornet, tuba, bass drum, trombone—and played the mule train into the square to the tune of 'The Campbells are coming'. In the square they obliged with ragged versions of 'God Save the King' and '*Deutschland Über Alles*'. Nasellino and the muleteers sneered and scuffed the white dust while the others stood to attention, sweaty with embarrassed pleasure. The last notes from the band were blaring out when a yell like a ship's siren drowned them; they subsided in a diminuendo of squeaks and moans.

'*Silenzio!*'

They fell silent, and turned to see the Countess standing at the corner of the street leading from the palazzo. She wore red beach pyjamas and a wide-brimmed straw hat.

'Good show,' Widdicombe said to Trommel. 'Here comes Sismonda at last.'

She moved slowly forward, her face flushed and her mouth set; the villagers fell back in awe as she passed Widdicombe and Trommel without speaking; instead she went up to Nasellino and addressed a few icy words to him. He replied in his villainous dialect, and the Countess stamped her foot, turning to the soldiers with a face which flamed from red to magenta to puce.

Major Widdicombe was saying with off-hand modesty, Trommel smirking cheerily at his side, 'Well, here we are, Sismonda. Found the old mules . . .' Then he noticed her expression and said, 'Good lord, you don't look at all well. What's up?'

The Countess exhaled like the gas blasting out of a captive balloon.

'Dolts!' she shrieked. 'If your brains were your bodies you would never cast a shadow: *these are the wrong mules!*'

14

MAJOR WIDDICOMBE stared at the Countess, rubbing at the stubble on his slack jaw.

'The wrong mules?' he said at length, blankly.

'Idiots!' said the Countess. 'These men are black marketeers. They have nothing whatever to do with Borgo San Marco. *Porca miseria!* You and your cloth-headed companions can do nothing right.'

Widdicombe tightened his lips and drew his revolver.

'We'll see about that,' he said, and turned to Trommel.

'I'm going to commandeer these barrels. You tell that chap Nasellino I'm confiscating his freight, and then tell him and his ruffians to make themselves scarce. I'll let' em keep the mules if they'll go quietly; if they won't, I'll take the mules as well.'

Major Trommel shrugged, and then spoke sharply to Nasellino, who replied by leaping in the air with a yell, drawing a knife and opening the blade with his teeth. Major Widdicombe fired a shot into the ground at the man's feet, and he dropped the knife.

'Now unload those mules,' Major Widdicombe said to the soldiers: puffing and grunting, they lifted off the barrels and laid them by the side of the mules in the white dust, the crowd murmuring and quacking excitedly.

'What are you doing now, prince of fools?' the Countess asked, but Widdicombe ignored her.

'Get moving!' he snapped at Nasellino, who glared at him briefly, said something with venom, and then motioned to his men; they marched out of the square and down the road with the mules while the villagers jeered and shouted after them.

'What did he say?' Widdicombe asked the Countess.

'That he would not sleep until your corpse was laid out in this square for him to dance on. And I do not wonder.'

Widdicombe snorted and said to her triumphantly, 'Well then. We may have got the wrong mules, but at least we found some oil for you. Look.'

He fired at one of the barrels, and the crowd gasped. A thin, colourless liquid spouted out of the hole in the barrel; Major Widdicombe stared at it dubiously.

'Doesn't look much like oil to me,' he said.

'Of course it is not oil!' the Countess screamed. 'Did I not say you can do nothing right? It is grappa!'

Major Widdicombe stood to one side, then bent down and applied his mouth to the stream of liquid; he shot upright gasping, and tugged the barrel over so that the hole lay uppermost.

'Phoo!' he said. 'Proof spirit. Grappa, do you call it? I'm most terribly sorry, Sismonda. We went through hell and high water to find that oil, and now it isn't oil at all. Trommel old egg, tell your man Wohlhaber to fetch the innkeeper with some taps and spigots.'

'Certainly, Major,' said Trommel, calling for Wohlhaber. 'But may I ask what you have in mind?'

'You may indeed. We'll get the cooker out here, and all the rations in store, and then the whole village is going to have a feast. I tell you, ancient Rome won't be in it.'

Major Trommel said, 'Well, you are burning your boats, but the villagers will thank you from the heart of their bottoms.'

*   *   *

It was dark, and a bonfire roared in the square; the brass band played; the villagers sang and danced with the soldiers. Private Dorbell disengaged himself from the grasp of a fat woman and went to the barrels.

'I'm thirsty,' he said to Corporal White, who was standing by a barrel looking owlishly around.

'Seen ole Filly anywhere?' he said. 'I've loss ole Fillermeena and I carn find her.'

'No, I haven't. I'm thirsty,' Dorbell said. 'Is that stoof any good?'

Corporal White said, 'It's just the bleeding job, Knocker, take my word for it.'

Dorbell drifted over to the long trestle tables where all the food had been laid out and was now reduced to crumbs and fragments. He found a glass, tripped over somebody who was asleep under the table with his legs sticking out, and went back to Corporal White; the singing had broken out loudly behind them, and Dorbell had to speak up to make himself heard.

'Give us some of that stoof, Corp.'

Corporal White teetered to a barrel and drew a glass of the grappa, handing it to Dorbell. He sipped.

'It tases funny,' he said, then drank, coughing and sawing at the air with his free hand. 'Hor!'

Corporal White said, 'It's only the first mouthful feels like that. You have some more, go on.'

Dorbell finished the glass and sat down heavily on the ground; White took his glass and topped it up.

'There you are,' he said. 'Do you a power of good.'

Private Dorbell sipped, sniffed, and said, 'I've broke me heart, Corp.'

'That's going to cure it at the double,' said Corporal White. 'Aye-aye, there's Filly dancing with some Eyetie bloke. I'll soon winkle her away from him: tell him it's a gentlemen's excuse-me,' and he vanished into the reeling, singing throng.

Dorbell coughed, seeing in the firelight only the scissoring legs of the dancers through the dust they were kicking up, and finished his second large glass of grappa.

'Broke me heart,' he said, a tear running down his cheek. Then he rose unsteadily to his feet, glaring across the crowd at the brass band.

'Listen to him. Got no idea,' he said, and filled another glass, took a swig and walked miraculously through the crowd in a straight line, without being so much as bumped on the way. He reached the tuba player and tapped him on the shoulder. The man stopped playing and looked inquiringly at Dorbell.

'Here, give us a lend of that,' Dorbell said, holding out his hands.

The tuba player smiled and handed over the instrument, then took off his cap and wiped a shiny bald head. Red lights gleamed from the brass. Dorbell solemnly and hygienically dipped the mouthpiece of the tuba in his glass, set the glass down, and picked up the tuba. He began to play *con amore*, and was soon surrounded by an admiring group of villagers. He could not see them very clearly, but was enjoying himself greatly, and had quite forgotten that he had broken his heart.

*   *   *

In the kitchen of the palazzo a barrel of grappa stood on the table, next to it an almost empty jug. Major Trommel

163

and Major Widdicombe faced each other across the table, toasted each other with studied gravity, and drank.

'Got to see Sismonda now,' Widdicombe said. 'Got to make her choose.'

Trommel nodded, sitting very erect with his eyes round and glassy.

'Should we go alone, or both together?'

'Together, eh? Then each of us'll see fair play.'

'Very well,' said Major Trommel and stood up, holding the edge of the table.

'We'll take this along,' Widdicombe said, picking up the jug and refilling it. 'You bring three glasses.'

In the big bedroom with the painted ceiling the Countess sat at her dressing table, her make-up streaked with tears and her hands clasped beneath her chin. She saw in the mirror the men come in, treading with exaggerated care, but did not turn round.

Major Widdicombe coughed.

'May we come in?'

'You *are* in,' the Countess pointed out, still gazing into the mirror.

'Yes, well,' Widdicombe said, finding himself at a loss or words. But he thought, Heavens above, she looks a bit of an old sack, must be a trick of the light.

Trommel said, 'Sismonda, you should not be moping here all alone. We have brought some grappa and some glasses. Come now,' and he placed a glass at her elbow; Major Widdicombe filled it from the jug.

The Countess turned round and said tragically, 'Of course I should be alone here. What else can a woman do but sit and weep when she is full of sadness? Tomorrow the communists will come, and then I shall be dead. And whose fault is that?'

She took a long drink, shuddering; Widdicombe patted

her on the back and said reassuringly, 'Now don't you worry about that. We're battle-hardened men now: if those ruddy communists come to Borgo San Marco they'll get more than they've bargained for. Come on, Sismonda, drink up.'

Widdicombe poured drinks for himself and Trommel, then sat with a thump on the bed. The Countess drank her grappa and said, 'You mean well, of course, both of you.' And then she said, 'But I could hang you from the palazzo wall by your toes and sign my name on your hides with a white-hot iron.'

'Hard words butter no parsnips,' Major Trommel said. 'We have been captured by communists, by—hrrm, partisans, we have rescued a mule train from a band of brigands, and all for you. We did it for love of you, do you understand? Is that not so, Major Widdicombe?'

'What? Oh yes,' Widdicombe said. 'Thass right.'

Major Trommel filled up the glasses, raising his own to Widdicombe.

'May the best man win,' he said, clinking glasses. They drank, and then turned back to the Countess. Major Widdicombe nudged Trommel.

'Berrer kneel down,' he said. 'Always kneel down when proposing, I think.'

'Quite right,' Major Trommel said.

They knelt together before the Countess. Widdicombe cleared his throat.

'We have come,' he said, 'both together because we are comrades even though we are supposed to be emenies, I mean fighting each other, because it would be a jolly bad show if one us were to sneak in by himself, I mean to say taking unfair advantage, because . . .'

He stopped, having lost the thread of his discourse.

Major Trommel said, 'We have come to ask you to

choose between us, Sismonda. I want to marry you, and so does Major Widdicombe.'

The Countess looked at them as they knelt, then drew back her head and laughed uproariously, her shoulders shaking and her thighs pressed together; Trommel and Widdicombe instinctively checked their flies, found all in order, and looked at each other in bewilderment.

The laughter turned to giggles, and finally the Countess regained control of herself.

'You!' she said cruelly. 'You pair of mountebanks, you donkeys chasing mules! You should see yourselves kneeling there like a couple of unfrocked priests! Do you for one moment imagine that I, Sismonda Giulietta Maria Francesca di San Marco, would choose for my husband either a thin dried-up old fool, or a fat young blubber-headed fool? Even fools have their uses at times, and so I worked upon you both to make you two fools go out and find the oil, but you were too foolish even to do that properly. If I marry again, it will be to a real man. Why, I tell you frankly, Major Trommel's servant is a better man than either of you, and if it had not been for his consolations at the time when I was sickening myself by offering my favours to you fools, I should have gone mad. Now get out and leave me in peace, fools!'

They rose slowly to their feet and left the bedroom, walking cataleptically down the passage; they went downstairs into the kitchen, through into the courtyard and out into the street through the carriage-arch without speaking. In the street they paused, scarcely hearing the sounds of revelry from the square.

Major Trommel said, 'Tomorrow remind me to shoot Wohlhaber.'

Widdicombe frowned.

'No, don't do that. Wohlhaber's not to blame. It's

her, don't you see? She got her claws into Wohlhaber too.'

'You are correct,' Major Trommel said, crying a little. 'She has corrupted him, my poor faithful servant.'

They walked down to the square and looked on at the firelit dancing and singing, standing glumly at the end of the street.

'Fools,' Widdicombe said tonelessly. 'That's what she said we were: just a pair of fools.'

Major Trommel said, 'It always hurts to have one's proposal rejected, sometimes more than others. The last time I proposed was in Bavaria, to a widow who kept a little inn. I sang my serenade to a mandolin as she sat on her balcony, and afterwards I proposed to her, suggesting that she might throw me a flower in token of her love. She did. In a big wooden tub.'

They crossed the square to the tables, found drinks and carried them to the parapet, sipping and staring into the blackness of the plain.

'Funny thing,' Widdicombe said idly, 'no firing going on down there: it's all quiet. They must be regrouping.'

Major Trommel turned and looked over the crowd, saying, 'Your private soldier is enjoying himself at all events.'

Dorbell was sweating and the tuba was grunting, people around him clapping and cheering. Widdicombe said, 'So are all these folk. We didn't find the oil, but they're well oiled, come to think of it. Plenty of food and heaps to drink: I bet there's never been such a night since the war started.'

They brightened, and Trommel said, 'Let us forget Sismonda. The night is young and the wine is red—at least, it is grappa, but you know what I mean. Let us enjoy ourselves also. We will drink some more, and then we will dance, and not once will we think of tomorrow. Agreed, Major?'

Widdicombe said, 'Well, at the moment I feel a bit like a whore at a Darby and Joan Club picnic. But I'll try. Yes, I'll certainly try.'

*   *   *

Still carrying the tuba, whose owner lay sleeping on the ground, Private Dorbell left the weary band thumping and wheezing still, and threaded his way through the few indefatigable dancers who had not yet succumbed to love or grappa. He noticed that the officers were among them, each dancing happily with a young peasant woman, and Sergeant Entwistle was clumping about with Gina; Corporal White was nowhere to be seen. Dorbell reeled up the street and into the palazzo, the tuba clanking against the table as he groped through the dark kitchen and into the corridor beyond, looking for Wohlhaber and improvising as he went, notes of melancholy flatulence echoing from the stone walls in the gloom.

He found Wohlhaber asleep by candlelight in his tiny room, lying fully clothed on his bed with the terra cotta vase of artificial flowers clutched to his chest, an empty jug overturned on the floor with a shattered glass beside it.

'Fritz!' said Dorbell. 'Wake up, Fritz!'

Wohlhaber slept on. Dorbell emitted a bass roar from the tuba, but the sleeping man moved not a muscle in response.

'Droonk as a fiddler's bitch,' Dorbell said disgustedly, and left the room, playing 'Rock of Ages'. Along the passage he saw a faint red light from an open door, and went towards it. The notes of the tuba ceased abruptly as he stood looking into a room with a painted ceiling; the light from the bonfire in the square flickered in it, and on the enormous bed a great mound of bedclothes heaved, a sobbing noise coming muffled from beneath them. Dorbell staggered forward and patted the mound with a tentative hand.

'There there, then,' he said.

At the sound of his voice the Countess's tousled head emerged from the bedclothes.

'You!' she said. 'It was you making that noise like an irrabiated *ippopotamo*. I have been frightened out of my skin. And it was you all the time.'

'It was me chooba,' Dorbell said literally. 'I couldn't do that by meself. But I'm sorry if it scared you.'

The Countess sighed and sat up blinking, one breast bare in the fitful firelight; Private Dorbell's jaw dropped. Casually the Countess adjusted her nightdress.

'Have a drink,' she said, and got out of bed, moving across the room past Dorbell and leaving a heady, musky scent to assail his nostrils; at the dressing table she turned.

'What would you like?' she asked.

Dorbell said, 'All that blowing's made me thirsty, but I'm dead fed up of that lighter fuel they call grappa. I'd like a bottle of pop if you've got one, mam.'

She said, 'I have some gin. Major Widdicombe thinks it has all gone, but I have been keeping a little for emergencies. And this may well turn out to be an emergency. . . . Where are the officers?'

'Down there dancing,' Dorbell said, pointing in the general direction of the square.

'And Wohlhaber?'

'Fast asleep. He won't come round for hours and hours.'

Decisively the Countess poured two glasses of gin and held one out to Private Dorbell, standing as close to him as the tuba permitted.

Dorbell said desperately, 'Shall I play you summat, mam?'

He drained the gin at one gulp, coughed and blew, his eyes watering.

'No,' she said quietly. 'Put that thing down.'

Dorbell said, 'I'll just play you "Brother James's Air". It's a very soothing piece.'

He played, and the Countess watched steadily until he had finished.

'Did you like it?'

'So beautiful,' she said. 'You are an artist.'

Dorbell blushed, and the Countess asked, 'What is your name?'

'It's Dorbell, mam.'

'No, no: your first name.'

'Well,' he said. 'They all call me Knocker, but me real name's Fred. Short for Frederick.'

'Ah!' the Countess breathed. 'Frederick. But that is Federico in Italian! My Federico!' and she burst into tears, going to the bed and sitting on it in a gale of sobbing. Dorbell stared at her with a moment's indecision, then put down the tuba carefully on the floor.

He went over to the Countess and said, 'Don't fret, lass. What is it? What's up, then?'

'I am so unhappy,' the Countess wailed.

Dorbell made clucking noises for a while, patting the woman on the head, and eventually he heaved her sideways on the bed and tucked her in.

'Do not go,' she said. 'Do not leave me. I am so lonely!'

Dorbell said, 'Aye, all right. You're lornly? I know what that's like. I'll stop a bit if you want.'

He took off his boots and rolled into bed with her, holding her hand until at length she gave a contented murmur and said, 'You are the only one.'

'Eh?'

'The only one I have ever met who is willing to be a comfort and not wish for anything else.'

Sleepily Dorbell said, 'Well I wouldn't be too sure of that. I can be a bit of a dog and all. But I'm dead tired, and it's nice and comfy like this, intit?'

'Federico,' she sighed, and they slept like children.

15

MAJOR WIDDICOMBE had fallen asleep in the square with his head on the warm and comfortable lap of a girl named Lea, both of them having sunk to the ground in stupefaction during the small hours. But as he swam with difficulty up into consciousness in the dazzle of early sunlight he became aware that his head was on hard ground, that there was a gong beating inside it, that his mouth and throat were apparently made of sandpaper, and that somebody was kicking him in the ribs. He opened his eyes and saw with clarity a black lace-up boot, calf length, then a pair of dirty corduroy breeches, a tattered jacket, a red scarf, a black beard, and a pair of little bloodshot eyes looking down at him: Martello. Major Widdicombe groaned and tried to get to his feet. Both hands had been tied in front of him, and he had some difficulty. He rolled over into a kneeling position, seeing Nasellino grinning with vindictive pleasure behind Martello, his earrings shaking. Then Widdicombe managed to struggle upright, his head opening and shutting to the accompaniment of thunderclaps. Some yards away stood Trommel, guarded and similarly bound.

Martello said, 'So you are awake, defiler of Italian youth, robber, capitalist grafter. You escaped us once, but you will not do so again. We have come to scorch out the whole befouled nest that is Borgo San Marco. The people shall triumph!'

'Ouch!' Major Widdicombe said, experimenting and finding it hard to rub his head with both wrists tied together. 'Either shoot me at once, or give me some aspirin.'

*   *   *

Dorbell was watching the Countess asleep by his side, and thinking, Well, I *was* a bit of a dog after all, this morning, eee she's nice, that she is, wants somebody to loook after her.

The Countess stirred, said, 'Mmm,' and opened her eyes, then sat up and stretched with lazy contentment. She stroked Dorbell's cheek and said, 'Oh, my Federico, never was I so happy! You are so strong and yet so tender, so masterful and yet so considerate.'

'Am I?' Dorbell said, surprised. 'I never knew that.'

'What were you before the war came, Federico?'

Dorbell said, 'I was a heavy coil winder in a factory.'

'Do you want to go back to England when the war is over and be a—a heavy coil winder again?'

'I don't that,' said Dorbell emphatically. 'It's a dreary job, dreary. And another thing. Aggie Bircumshaw's waiting for me back home.'

'Who?'

'A lass I used to know. I hope I never see her again.'

The Countess said, 'If I have my way, you will not. Come, Federico, a kiss!'

'Me mouth feels like a chicken-run,' Dorbell said, fending her off affectionately. 'Give us a minute to wash and take a sup of water, and then we'll have a bit of a cuddle if you want.'

He kissed her ear and got out of bed, putting on his socks

and trousers, humming. He was standing at the washbasin when the communist partisans burst into the room.

*   *   *

Corporal White groaned and shifted position, Filomena's hair across his face and in his open mouth, tickling and irritating him. He mumbled something incoherent, shoving the girl's knee off his stomach, then slid out of bed with his eyes closed, ungumming them as his feet touched the floor. He put on singlet and trousers, then moved sleep-walking to the handbasin and washed, grunting from time to time. He came fully awake and grinned, glancing back at the sleeping Filomena. Those bleeding mules, he thought. If it hadn't been for them I'd still be chasing that bit of crumpet, it's an ill wind, all right all right. Today's a new day, and you never know what it's going to bring: ding-dong, driver, *I'm* on the bus.

Five minutes later he and Filomena were hustled out into the corridor by three armed partisans to join Dorbell and the Countess, Sergeant Entwistle and Gina. The two servant girls were weeping and threatening hysterics, but the Countess was composed, though pale. They were all marched down into the square where Widdicombe and Trommel stood side by side under guard, and the villagers watched with impassive faces.

One of the partisans came to Martello and said, 'This is the lot, comrade. There's no one left in the palazzo except for a dead man.'

'A dead man?'

'Yes, comrade. He's lying there dead as a doornail, with a pot of flowers on his chest.'

'Good,' said Martello. 'Excellent. I see that tables have been most considerately provided. I shall stand on one, and that woman'—he pointed to the Countess—'on another, and after I have addressed the people, we shall hang her from the lamp-post. Then the others, one by one. You will see, comrades, after the example we shall set today, everyone in the village will vote for the workers' party.'

They stood the Countess, still in her nightdress, on one table beneath the lamp-post, and Martello mounted the other while the partisans yelled for silence at the crowd, whose members were already silent, holding their heads and peering from bleary eyes. Martello began his speech, and went on for a very long time; when at last he finished, the crowd rustled with relief. One of the partisans produced a length of rope, tied a noose at one end, and cast the other over the crossbar of the lamp-post. He slipped the noose over the Countess's neck.

She shouted, 'People of Borgo San Marco! Friends! Today this filth in red scarves has decreed that I must die. So be it. I would gladly die if it served any useful purpose. All I can do is ask you to believe that I have never broken faith with you.' She pointed to Major Widdicombe and Major Trommel. 'Those two men brought in the wrong mules. Do not judge them too harshly; at least they tried to save me. The mules and the oil will come, but I shall be gone. Remember me.'

Trommel said, 'This is all very well, but it does not alter the fact that our cook is goosed,' and then fell silent as Dorbell shoved past the guard and climbed on to the table.

'You're a brave lass,' he said. 'I'll stop by you, and I'll go next.'

Four of the partisans tied more rope to the folding cross-members of the trestle table, then waited for Martello to give the signal to collapse it; others dragged Dorbell off it. Martello raised his hand; interested, Nasellino moved closer to watch the fun.

*   *   *

In the palazzo Private Wohlhaber opened his eyes, staring at the ceiling. He felt refreshed, in a state of pellucid calm, having slept through his hangover; his hands were stiff from clutching the vase, but that was all. He removed it from his chest, putting it carefully down at his bedside, then rose, flexing his fingers. He washed, brushed his teeth, shaved in cold water with grunts and grimaces, then dressed. Feeling the need of a cigarette, he hunted unsuccessfully through his pockets. *Macht nichts*, he thought, I'll get some from one of the Tommies. He left the room, but returned a few minutes later, puzzled: the palazzo was empty. Wohlhaber scratched his head, polished his boots meticulously, then picked up the pot of flowers and left the palazzo, walking idly down to the square. He stopped at the end of the street, seeing the Countess on the trestle table with the noose round her neck, and took in the situation at once. There was not an instant to spare, not a microsecond. With the face of a man about to sacrifice a newly-wedded wife or a first-born son, Wohlhaber hurled the thing as hard as he could.

The terra-cotta vase sailed through the air in a high parabola, falling directly on Martello's head and shattering. As Martello dropped to the ground amid the shards of the broken pot, overwhelming the flowers there fell a snow-storm of banknotes under and around and on top of Martello's unconscious figure. The breeze whirled the notes here and there, and Nasellino let out a shriek of greed, diving after them. The partisans who were holding the ropes dropped them incontinently and joined the others in the scramble; Dorbell leaped up on to the table and whipped the noose from the Countess's neck, hugging her briefly and then helping her down.

'Quick!' said Major Widdicombe to Major Trommel. 'You untie my hands and I'll untie yours.'

The square was in pandemonium as villagers joined the partisans, fighting and squabbling over the money. A banknote drifted the way of Private Wohlhaber; wryly he picked it up and stuffed it into his pocket, thinking, *Ach, so,* a consolation prize, and to tell the truth I was ashamed in the end that I sold their truck.

Trommel was fiddling with Major Widdicombe's bonds when there was a loud burst of firing from the road leading to the plain, and bullets zipped over the heads of the struggling crowd. Major Widdicombe's hands fell to his sides, free; he chafed them and looked up to see a jeep and two open trucks roar into the square, bristling with automatic weapons. The jeep held four immaculate soldiers in U.S. Army uniforms, three of whom wore spotless white helmets, the first truck held a group of men in overalls and paratroopers' helmets, and the second, the Amazons of the New Italy.

Major Trommel's hands were still bound. He and Widdicombe stared as the vehicles skidded to a standstill and their occupants jumped out, the Amazons and the paratroopers herding the partisans and Nasellino over against the parapet. Tina Menotti strode over to a thickset man with a hard, brick-red face and a U.S. colonel's uniform, who had leaped out of the jeep and was bending over Martello.

He said, 'Fractured skull. This guy'll be no good to anybody for a few months.'

Dorbell peered from the embrace of the Countess as Marta came past. He grinned in an embarrassed way, and Marta tossed her head, then gazed up proprietorially at the tall, ginger-haired paratrooper at her side.

Private Dorbell said to himself aloud in the moment before the Countess engulfed him again, 'Well, them paratroopers aren't the only ones to land on their feet.'

Tina Menotti said to the colonel, 'All in order, *colonello*,' and the man nodded, then sauntered over towards Widdicombe and Trommel, but the Countess ran between and intercepted him, Dorbell trailing behind. The colonel raised his eyebrows at sight of the Countess's nightdress, saw behind her the noose hanging from the lamp-post, and cocked his head at her.

'We were just in time, mam,' he said. 'Who are you, and who's this soldier?'

'I am the Countess of San Marco,' she said, 'and this is my Federico, my fiancé.'

'My God,' said the colonel, surprised. 'John Pfefferman, United States Army, at your service.'

Major Widdicombe came forward with Trommel and said indignantly, 'You spoiled it all. We were just turning the tables on them when you arrived. We could have done it by ourselves.'

Colonel Pfefferman grimaced. He glanced round the square: the villagers were standing with hands clasped over their pockets, not a banknote in sight, and the communist partisans stood by the parapet with their hands on their heads, gazing fearfully at the automatic weapons menacing them.

'Oh, sure,' he said to Widdicombe. 'I've heard all about you.'

Major Widdicombe said, 'I don't like your tone of voice. There's a whole plot in operation by these communists . . .'

Colonel Pfefferman cut him off.

'We know all about that, too,' he said. 'That's been nipped in the bud.' He pointed at Trommel. 'This guy your prisoner?'

Major Trommel said, 'Yes, I am. The major has been prevented from taking me to his headquarters by the confused situation in the plain, is that not so, Major Widdi-combe?'

Widdicombe nodded, full of gratitude.

'I have news for you,' Colonel Pfefferman said drily. 'The situation in the plain is far from confused. In fact, the war in Italy is over. Your Eighth Army's way up beyond Klagenfurt and high-tailing it north to meet up with the Russians. You're going to have some explaining to do when you make it back to your unit.'

Widdicombe and Trommel were staring at each other aghast, remembering the preternatural quietness in the plain during the night, and the Countess said, '*È finita, la guerra?*' A villager nearby overheard this, the word ran through the square like a flame through dry bracken, and in no time at all everyone was shouting and cheering. Widdicombe shook his head in puzzlement.

'Anyway,' he said, 'we were in the interior. It's thanks to us that this communist business has been stopped. And I don't speak Italian. Major Trommel overheard all about the plot. You must have met Spud Henryson. But let me tell you, you've got Major Trommel to thank as well as me.'

Through the uproar Colonel Pfefferman said with con-tempt, 'Don't kid yourself, Major. This is an American operation. We stopped the reds, and we rescued you. Think it over. I'm a colonel in a real army, and you're a major in the good Lord knows what. This is an all-American job, I'm getting the credit for it, and it's going to stay that way.'

'It isn't fair,' Major Widdicombe said, wounded. People were embracing the newly arrived soldiers, holding hands and dancing with one another; he looked at the grinning paratroopers, the gay blue-scarved Amazons, and appealed to the Countess: 'You can tell him what we've done.'

She smiled sweetly and said, 'Do you really want me to do that?'

Widdicombe hesitated, and Major Trommel said, 'Perhaps not, on second thoughts. But we . . .'

He stopped speaking: strange sounds could be heard through the general jubilant din. All heads turned to face the road leading down into the plain, and then a string of mules came into sight, laden with barrels. They were not Nasellino's mules, and the five muleteers attending them were strangers. Escorting them were three American soldiers, Lieutenant Henryson at their head. The noise of jubilation redoubled.

The Countess screamed, 'It is the mules! *Mamma mia*, the mules are here!'

Colonel Pfefferman smiled broadly; the villagers were running to meet the mule train, yelling and gesticulating. In the background the brass band assembled, an angry tuba player coming over to Dorbell and haranguing him about his missing tuba; the Countess soothed him and told him it was in her bedroom at the palazzo. He ran off after the instrument, while the rest of the band struck up raggedly.

'We picked up the mules a couple of miles back,' Pfefferman said. 'I put a guard on them, and I thought I'd let Henryson bring them in; it's no more than his due.' He looked at Major Widdicombe and said, 'Sure, it was Henryson who tipped us off about the rising. He'll get a medal for this: I'll see to it personally.' He smiled again. 'I'll make brigadier-general too. It's a great life, Major.'

Widdicombe said, 'Well, you rotten dog.'

Pfefferman said, 'I'll report that in due course. Or maybe I'll let it ride. It doesn't mean a thing, coming from a fool like you. We'll clear up here and put Henryson in charge with the parachute boys and their girl-friends. They should have quite a time. You and your clowns and your fool prisoner be ready to pull out in twenty minutes.'

He turned on his heel and said to the Countess, 'I'll take you back to your home, mam. It may be quite some time before you see your fiancé again.'

The Countess flung her arms round Dorbell's neck and kissed him.

'Federico,' she said. 'Come back to me, my love!'

'I'll do that all right,' Dorbell said. 'Goodbye, duck. I'll come back as soon as they let me out.'

Wohlhaber came over and stood by Major Trommel.

He said, 'Beg to report, sir, I stole the Tommies' truck.'

'Clear off, will you?' Major Widdicombe said, understanding nothing. 'Go and comfort Dorbell or something. Major Trommel and I wish to be alone.'

Wohlhaber looked blank; Trommel snapped at him in German, and then he went away.

Four soldiers were carrying Martello to a truck. The fat woman in black watched them, the little girl at her side, then bent down, rummaging among the fragments of the terra cotta vase. She gathered the artificial flowers into a grotesque bunch, took the girl by the hand and dragged her after Colonel Pfefferman, halting him and smiling proudly as the little girl curtsied and held out the flowers. Pfefferman took them, glanced at them disparagingly and then dropped them in the dust, walking on with the Countess and wiping his hand as he went. The fat woman burst into tears.

Colonel Pfefferman's penetrating voice came through a sudden lull in the noise. He was orating at the Countess as they walked, small flecks of spittle at the corners of his mouth:

'You'll see, mam. We'll have this operation tied up in Europe in a week or two, by God, and then we're going to light out and finish those goddam Nips. You'll see. . . .'

The voice died away soon afterwards. Widdicombe and Trommel faced each other.

Widdicombe said, 'We could still do something. The credit *is* ours, or most of it.'

'Yes,' said Trommel, glancing over at Henryson. 'But he is not a bad young fellow, that one. He is based on Tunis, do you remember? There could be great troubles for him if you take matters any further. As it is, he will be a hero, medal and all.'

'Say nothing, you mean?'

They looked at each other, and then both nodded.

Major Widdicombe said heavily, 'That's that, then. So it all came to nothing, all we ever did. Here, let me untie your hands.'

He loosed the bonds, and Trommel said, 'Thank you, Major. . . . No. I do not think it all came to nothing.'

'Why not? They all think we're just a pair of fools.'

Major Trommel said, 'In a madhouse a sane man is abnormal. They have their war; let them keep it. The medals and the citations, they are for others, not for us. But you and I. . . . Remember, before this, there was a brass band for us, and there was dancing.'

'You're right,' Widdicombe said.

'Let them think us fools. You and I—we can salute each other in honour and dignity.'

Which is what they did.

Also available in Arrow Books by W. H. Canaway . . .

CROWS IN A GREEN TREE

Pym Hallett, a huge, handsome twenty-year-old employed as a farm-hand, is the last of a line going back a thousand years. His father is lord of the manor. But as well as winning the V.C. in the war, Hallett Senior was forced by the untimely arrival of Pym to marry a wife so young that she might have been Pym's sister. The father's indiscretions continue to plague the son, who falls in and out of affairs on his own account and can seldom resolve his conflicts. But when the seductive, Italian-born Gianna becomes entangled simultaneously with Halletts Senior *and* Junior, it's a question of the survival of the fittest . . . .

THE GREY SEAS OF JUTLAND

At the turn of the century in England, the Wynne family, like so many others, are heedless of the shadows cast by the coming war. George Wynne's father wants his son to follow him into the Church, but George insists on entering the Navy.

Whilst staying with his German cousin, Werner, George meets Claire and her mother, touring Europe from America. And so, at the same time that national rivalry is approaching its tragic climax, George and Werner also enter into a rivalry of their own.

As England's pastoral scene is shattered by the First World War, so George and Werner finally face each other at the Battle of Jutland, here described in masterly and gripping narrative.

RECENT GENERAL FICTION FROM ARROW

2001: A SPACE ODYSSEY   Arthur C. Clarke

The dramatic novel of one of the most spectacular films ever produced, based on the screenplay by Stanley Kubrick and Arthur C. Clarke.

COVENANT WITH DEATH   John Harris

A novel that depicts the appalling realism of war: the carnage, the wholesale slaughter, the nightmare stink of cordite . . .

KICK TURN   Anthony Glyn

A witty and penetrating account of a rather naive young man's discovery of women . . .

THE ROBBERS PASSING BY
George Malcolm Thomson

Illicit affairs and political scandal in gossip-column London.

TALL, BALDING, THIRTY-FIVE Anthony Firth

'Beyond doubt, the wittiest and most original first crime story for a long time.' (*The Sunday Times*)

THE HOUND OF HEAVEN James Dillon White

Bloodshed, torture and sexual passion in a Latin-American revolution.

STRANGE EVIL   Jane Gaskell

The controversial first novel by an equally controversial writer.

THE DEEP SILENCE — Douglas Reeman

A magnificent story of men and ships at sea, set in the Far East in the near future.

WITCH BANE — Robert Neill

Witchcraft and paganistic rites in Cromwell's England at the time of the Civil War.

THE WAR QUEEN — J. F. Broxholme

Boadicea—and the spring of terror that decided the fate of Roman rule in Britain.

LIGHT CAVALRY ACTION — John Harris

A magnificent cliff-hanger about an action for libel—by a General against his former subordinate.

THE GREEKS HAVE A WORD FOR IT — Barry Unsworth

Two men arrive in Athens on the same ship: and at the end of this highly-amusing novel, only one of them is left alive.

RITUAL — David Pinner

Murder, paganism and Midsummer Night orgies in a Cornish village.

THE SPINSTERS — John Williams

One woman's bid for hatred—and another's for love.

SEVEN BEDS TO CHRISTMAS — Ian Rodger

Sweden in winter—and one man's adventures in search of a bed.

THE RENDEZVOUS — Evelyn Anthony

Twenty years after war's end, Terese Masson meets her former interrogator, now a hunted Nazi war criminal.

THE SCARPERER — Brendan Behan

A novel by the author of *Borstal Boy*, in the true, uproarious Behan tradition.

THE WOMAN IN MY LIFE — Ludwig Bemelmans

Tender, touching, full of shrewd philosophy, the voice of Bemelmans is heard again in this, perhaps his most delightful novel.

THE ROMANTIC EGOISTS — Louis Auchincloss

By the author of *The Rector of Justin* and one of the leading writers in America today.

THE HOUSE PARTY — David Walder

A magnificently funny novel stirred into a sizzling cocktail for those who cannot take their politicians neat!

THE FAIR LADIES OF SALAMANCA — David Walder

An untimely affair and a brother-officer's death put his own Army career in jeopardy.

THE SPANISH FARM — R. H. Mottram

The classic from the First World War, recently televised on BBC 2, with a preface by John Galsworthy.

THE YEAR OF THE HORSETAILS
R. F. Tapsell

A magnificent novel set on a grand scale about the marauding nomads of the steppe-lands of Eurasia.

CONSTANTINE
Frank G. Slaughter

The dramatic story of Constantine the Great's stormy life in the turbulent Roman world of the 3rd and 4th centuries.

THE PROMISE
Pearl S. Buck

A story of love in war, of a promise fulfilled and a promise betrayed.

THE DAM
Paul Ferris

A tense and authentic novel of sabotage in the Welsh hills.

THE PRESIDENT IS DEAD
Philippe Alexandre

What would happen in France if the French President died leaving no obvious choice for a successor?

THY TEARS MIGHT CEASE
Michael Farrell

'A work of real splendour and heroic size.' (Kenneth Allsop, *The Daily Mail*).

A WREN CALLED SMITH
Alexander Fullerton

A tough and racy story of love and war at sea, by the author of *Surface!*

Recent General Non-Fiction from Arrow:

THE PLOUGH BOY: Tony Parker

A true account of a murder, committed at Clapham Common in 1953, and a trial.

'OLD ROWLEY': Dennis Wheatley

The famous novelist's account of the very private life of Charles II.

I SEARCH FOR RAINBOWS: Barbara Cartland

The autobiography of the celebrated romantic novelist.

TO AUNTIE WITH LOVE: Jack de Manio

An hilarious chronicle of all the awful things which have ever happened in Broadcasting House.

THE MAN FROM MOSCOW: Greville Wynne

A personal account of one of the most famous and publicised spy cases of the century.

THE CRIME OF MARY STUART:
George Malcolm Thomson

A murder of the 1560s that nothing of the 1960s could match.

ARROW BOOKS—Publishers of the World-famous

DENNIS WHEATLEY

Famous Black Magic Stories:

    THE SATANIST

    THE DEVIL RIDES OUT

    TO THE DEVIL—A DAUGHTER

    THE HAUNTING OF TOBY JUGG

    STRANGE CONFLICT

    THE KA OF GIFFORD HILLARY

    THEY USED DARK FORCES

Roger Brook Novels:

    THE LAUNCHING OF ROGER BROOK

    THE SHADOW OF TYBURN TREE

    THE RISING STORM

    THE MAN WHO KILLED THE KING

    THE DARK SECRET OF JOSEPHINE

    THE RAPE OF VENICE

    THE SULTAN'S DAUGHTER

    THE WANTON PRINCESS

Duke de Richleau Stories:

THE PRISONER IN THE MASK

VENDETTA IN SPAIN

THE SECOND SEAL

THREE INQUISITIVE PEOPLE

THE FORBIDDEN TERRITORY

THE GOLDEN SPANIARD

CODEWORD—GOLDEN FLEECE

STRANGE CONFLICT

DANGEROUS INHERITANCE

Gregory Sallust Adventures:

BLACK AUGUST

CONTRABAND

THE ISLAND WHERE TIME STANDS STILL

THE SCARLET IMPOSTOR

FAKED PASSPORTS

THE BLACK BARONESS

V FOR VENGEANCE

COME INTO MY PARLOUR

TRAITORS' GATE

FAMOUS AUTHORS PUBLISHED BY ARROW BOOKS

Evelyn Anthony

Louis Auchincloss

Nigel Balchin

Lillian Beckwith

Brendan Behan

Ludwig Bemelmans

Ursula Bloom

Pearl S. Buck

Patrick Campbell

W. H. Canaway

Barbara Cartland

Eustace Chesser

Alan Clark

Arthur C. Clarke

John Creasey

Michael Farrell

C. S. Forester

Alexander Fullerton

Michael Green

John Harris

Eric Linklater

Ethel Mannin

Guy de Maupassant

Milena Milani

Penelope Mortimer

R. H. Mottram

Netta Muskett

Oluf Reed Olsen

Douglas Reeman

Denise Robins

Simenon

Frank G. Slaughter

Bram Stoker

Arthur Swinson

Christopher Sykes

John Terraine

Edgar Wallace

Colin Wilson

Godfrey Winn

Greville Wynne

Andrew York

Emile Zola

and also the world-famous DENNIS WHEATLEY, 'Prince of Thriller-Writers'